MOUNTAIN UPSIDE DOWN

MOUNTAIN UPSIDE DOWN

SARA RYAN

DUTTON CHILDREN'S BOOKS

DUTTON CHILDREN'S BOOKS
An imprint of Penguin Random House LLC
1745 Broadway, New York, New York 10019

First published in the United States of America by Dutton Children's Books,
an imprint of Penguin Random House LLC, 2025

Copyright © 2025 by Sara Ryan

Penguin Random House values and supports copyright.
Copyright fuels creativity, encourages diverse voices, promotes free speech
and creates a vibrant culture. Thank you for buying an authorized edition of this book
and for complying with copyright laws by not reproducing, scanning, or distributing
any part of it in any form without permission. You are supporting writers and allowing
Penguin Random House to continue to publish books for every reader. Please note
that no part of this book may be used or reproduced in any manner for the
purpose of training artificial intelligence technologies or systems.

Dutton is a registered trademark of Penguin Random House LLC.
The Penguin colophon is a registered trademark of Penguin Books Limited.

Visit us online at PenguinRandomHouse.com.

Library of Congress Cataloging-in-Publication Data is available.

ISBN 9780593699515
1   3   5   7   9   10   8   6   4   2

Printed in the United States of America

BVG

Design by Anna Booth
Text set in Adobe Caslon Pro

This book is a work of fiction. Any references to historical events,
real people, or real places are used fictitiously. Other names, characters, places,
and events are products of the author's imagination, and any resemblance to
actual events or places or persons, living or dead, is entirely coincidental.

The publisher does not have any control over and does not assume any
responsibility for author or third-party websites or their content.

FOR ELLEANOR,
WHO'S BEEN THERE SINCE WE WERE
THE SAME AGE AS ALEX AND PJ

I wish I was a hole in the ground
Wish I was a hole in the ground
If I was a hole in the ground
I'd be a mountain upside down
Wish I was a hole in the ground

—variation on "Mole in the Ground," traditional

PROLOGUE: LAST THURSDAY

IF YOU THINK ABOUT IT A CERTAIN WAY, IT should be easy to tell the person who's been your best friend since third grade that you like her.

Because you already know she likes you enough to be your best friend, right?

And you already talk about everything.

Well, almost everything.

We were in her yard, sitting on opposite ends of the widest, lowest-hanging branch of the dead-yet-sturdy barkless tree we always climb. I was leaning against the trunk with my knees pulled into my chest. PJ was farther out, straddling the branch with her legs dangling.

"So, um, I was wondering," I said, my face catching fire, "I mean I was wanting, I mean I am wanting, I mean I want— Argh!"

"Wait, don't finish!" PJ said.

I smashed my head into my knees and turned into wood and petrified.

Because I was still hiding my head, I felt, rather than saw, that PJ was scooting closer to me on the branch. "No no no, it's nothing bad! I just—I wanted to be the one to ask you! I had it all planned out!"

I unpetrified and managed to look at her. Not directly at her, but sort of at the general area of the branch where she was sitting, and then at a particular knot in the wood, which kind of looked like an eye, so it was *like* I was making eye contact? She kept talking: "But I think this is actually better, because I was pretty sure, but not exactly, like, two hundred percent sure?"

Then PJ got even closer, perching inches away from me. "Please," she said, "*go on*." She goofily drew out the last two words in a weird voice, and that made me laugh, which made me braver, so I said, "Okay, so I was going to ask if you wanted to, um, date? I mean, um, date me, specifically?"

"Yes!" PJ said. "That's almost how I was going to ask you, but I was going to say *girlfriend!* Do you want to be girlfriends? In a gay way?"

And then I was laughing again and PJ scooted even closer, and despite the whole sitting-in-a-tree-K-I-S-S-I-N-G thing, which makes you think that actually might be where you're supposed to be while you kiss? It is in reality extremely awkward to have your first kiss with your girlfriend while sitting in a tree.

But I would still recommend it.

ONE

"OH, ALEX, YOU JUST GET *RIGID*," GRANDMA said the last time it happened—"it" being how I sometimes freeze up and can't talk or move. It's been happening more often lately. That time it was because she wanted us to go to the new neighbors' down the street and introduce ourselves.

I know it's supposed to be good to know your neighbors, but I couldn't face knocking on a stranger's door. Especially because people always wonder right away why it's just me and Grandma who live in our house.

It makes me feel like we have to explain everything. How my mom died right after I was born, and how she and my dad weren't married, and how after a while my dad got married to someone else—I was still little—and they wanted custody of me, but Grandma wanted to keep me, I think maybe because of how much she misses my mom, and maybe also because of how much she misses my grandpa, who I never met because he had a heart attack and also died, way before I was born. Or maybe because she didn't think my dad and Laura would raise me the way she wanted me to be brought up. That makes her sound like she's constantly sad or overly controlling, and neither of those things are really true, at least not all the time. I see my dad and stepmom and half brothers every so often, but the way they're in my life seems more like how other people talk about their aunts and uncles who live far away. Like, maybe they care about them a lot, but when they get together, mostly what they do is eat and pose for pictures and watch sports and play games that mean they don't have to find too many things to talk about.

And I know we wouldn't really have to tell the new neighbors all of that? And in fact it'd be very weird if we did? But I just kept thinking about how they'd be staring and wondering, and I got rigid.

In the end Grandma went over there with some cookies, and I stayed home supposedly doing homework but actually mostly texting my girlfriend.

So far being PJ's girlfriend isn't very different from being her best friend, except that we hold hands a lot and sometimes kiss, and when we do, it feels fizzy and loud in my brain, like drinking the sugar soda Grandma refuses to buy and listening to an amazing song at the same time, only it's all happening in my head. Well, and technically in my lips. And my hands. And—anyway.

PJ's full name is Portia Jane Silverman. Her parents—she has two, Rachel and Kyla—are both professors at the community college. Rachel teaches music, and Kyla teaches communication studies. Actually they're both *adjunct* professors, a word I learned when they were yelling about adjunct salaries one time when I was at their house for a sleepover. I wonder what sleepovers will be like now? Will we even still be allowed to have them? Maybe I should tell PJ not to tell them that we're girlfriends, except she's probably already told them, because that family talks about everything. Except maybe she hasn't, because us being girlfriends is exactly the sort of thing Rachel and Kyla will think is so adorable, and they'll want to buy us, like, rainbow capes, which wouldn't be so bad except I'd rather have rainbow suspenders. Except the last time I wore suspenders, Jason Kruse snapped them like they were bra straps and then also snapped my bra straps.

Anyway I don't talk about my family too much, and by my family I mostly just mean Grandma, because Dad and Laura and the twins don't count, not in the same way. I try not to talk about anything I'm worried about, either, and by that I also mostly just mean Grandma, not that she's a thing, but she's what I'm worrying about a lot these days, and what really sucks is that if it were anything else, she'd be the person I'd want to tell about it.

I could tell PJ, I guess, but every time I think I might try, something stops me. Like, maybe I'm imagining it; most of the time Grandma seems like she always has. Except sometimes she'll do something like say she's never been to the restaurant we were just at last week, and yesterday she was looking through old photos and pointed to one of my mom and smiled at me and said, "That's you."

PJ AND I MET IN THIRD GRADE, BECAUSE

we were in the same group, a group of two, for a project where we were all doing different articles to make a tourist guide for where we live, Failin, Oregon, which, yes, everyone always makes the joke about adding a *g*, but it's literally just a person's last name. When we were working on it at PJ's house, Rachel said it was outrageous to have third graders produce bland propaganda, and that we should be looking into the continuing impact of the loss of timber industry jobs. Kyla said it was asking a lot for third graders to cover topics adults don't like to discuss, and Rachel sighed and said she had a point.

So we ended up writing about the Faithful Angus Antique Mall that had just opened. We thought it was interesting that the building had started out as one thing (a brewery) and became a different thing (an abandoned building that people graffitied and broke the windows of and I guess sometimes had parties in?) and was now a third thing.

And after we got Kyla to drive us there to take pictures, we liked the actual place, too. The first thing we saw was a framed black-and-white photo of Faithful Angus next to a plaque about the building history, and that's how we learned Faithful Angus was Hosiah Failin's dog.

Hosiah Failin supposedly "founded" Failin, and named it after himself of course, and that's what Claudia Wilford wrote about. PJ asked why Claudia left out the people who were already living there before it was called Failin, and Claudia said that the website she used didn't say anything about other people being there already, and PJ said she should have looked at more than one, and I said PJ was right, and that also did she know that Columbus didn't actually discover America, either? We got sent out in the hall for being disruptive, but it was the opposite of a punishment because we just whispered back and forth until the bell rang and have been best friends ever since.

If she shows up, I'll get to see PJ after school today, and also some other friends, because it's Tuesday, and that's the day for Youth Council. I first found out about Youth Council from Grandma, actually. She worked for FPL before she retired (FPL stands for Failin Public Library, but people who work there never say the whole name, so I don't, either), in Technical Services, which she said was the only part of the library that was ever even quiet anymore.

Technical Services is the basement room where stuff gets ordered, and also the place where once the stuff comes, it gets labeled so people know where it's supposed to go and barcoded so people can check it out. The room is divided up into a lot of cubicles, so when you stand at the top of the stairs about to go down to the basement, like I did when I visited Grandma at work, the room looks like a giant gray honeycomb. I liked seeing how people decorated their gray honeycomb cubicle cells. Grandma's had a big calendar with pictures of cats (cute), a lot of cartoons about libraries (some funny, some I didn't get), and a bunch of pictures of me (embarrassing). For a while someone had a huge bedsheet draped over their entire cubicle, which made it more like a sort of square tent. The sheet was patterned to look like the Milky Way, so the effect was really cool, and I always wanted to see what it was like inside, but Grandma said it would be invading their privacy.

Youth Council is basically the opposite of the gray Technical Services honeycomb. We meet in a literal storage closet (a really big closet, obviously, but still), we sit on the floor, and we are super loud.

On a normal Tuesday, I'd meet up with PJ at her locker, and we'd walk across School Street to the library together. (Yes, the school is on School Street. All the schools, actually—the elementary, middle, and high schools are all in a row. Failin names tend to be very obvious.)

But PJ told me at lunch that she couldn't come today. I asked why, and instead of telling me anything real, she just said, "Stuff," so I said okay and tried not to worry that it was something bad, or something to do with me, or both. But I couldn't eat anything afterward, and it turns out that one bite of a peanut butter and honey sandwich isn't a great lunch, no matter how long that bite takes you to chew.

When I get to the library, it's early, and Alonso, our librarian, is still on his lunch break—he eats at weird times because he works late—so the closet isn't unlocked yet, and I have to hide in the manga shelves from the Creeper. I don't know the Creeper's real name, nor do I want to. He's a security guard and he never talks to me, but I've caught him looking at me and it's creepy, therefore, he's the Creeper. I find the first volume of a series I haven't seen before, which never happens, so I start reading. It's another one set at some kind of special school, but I can't tell yet if the students will have magic or superpowers or just regular drama and, like, fashion issues.

"Hey," PJ says, bumping my shoulder with hers. I shove the book back onto the shelf, and we hug, and it's a stupidly huge relief to breathe in her lemony shampoo and raspberry lip balm and feel her arms around me. PJ swims and does push-ups for fun, so her arms are extremely strong.

"Hi!" I say, muffled into her neck. "I thought you had . . . stuff?"

"I do," she says. She stops hugging me and puts her hands in the pocket of her hoodie. "But it's going to be later, I guess."

"Is everything okay?"

She's already walking away.

ALONSO HAS PUT OUT THE PICNIC BLANket, which is still strongly orange-scented from two weeks ago when we were making bath bombs and someone knocked over the little bottle of essential oil, and no one noticed until it had soaked in. Fortunately, no one on Youth Council has scent sensitivity, and, as Faisal pointed out, there are a lot worse smells that could have gotten on it.

Yesenia says there's a video we all need to watch immediately. Alonso tells her to go ahead and hook up the laptop and projector. As long as the video is PG-13 and five minutes or less, we can discuss it for our icebreaker. Yesenia, me, PJ, Faisal, Linh, and Enrique have all been coming to Youth Council long enough that it doesn't seem like there should be any ice left to break. But then I think of all the things about me they don't know. There are probably just as many things I don't know about them.

The video is about a capybara and a spider monkey who are friends, and Yesenia says we all need to literally die from the cute. Enrique says she doesn't literally mean literally, and she says, "You got me, I want only you to literally die, Enrique, everyone else can just figuratively die, now shut up because the music is also really good, okay?"

We shut up and watch while we eat snacks. "These are the saddest snacks that ever snacked," says Linh. She has a point: to drink, there's slightly bluish water because the blue raspberry Gatorade powder is just about gone, and to eat, there are extremely dry and stale granola bars. But at least the granola bars are less messy than the cheese popcorn everyone likes that inevitably gets everywhere.

After the video, we work on cleaning the storytime toys so they'll be safe for babies to chew and drool on again, and we talk about why "two different species of animals are friends" is always so great. Linh says it's even better if the animals are really different sizes. I think about how PJ and I are really different sizes, too, and I can't decide if I want someone to point that out, because it would be a way to call us cute, but it would also be a way to call me fat. Which is true, but sometimes people say it like it's a synonym for disgusting. Even though I don't think anyone on Youth Council would.

I've lost the thread of what everyone's talking about, so I look over to Alonso. He has the half smile that means he's having fun with us but is also tired and maybe has a headache. He gets them a lot and is always trying new herbal remedies that smell . . . interesting.

"Is everything okay?" I ask, and remember a second after I do that it's the same question I asked PJ. Alonso doesn't answer me, either, and I wonder if my voice has suddenly stopped being audible to anyone but me, or if there's something wrong with that question, and then I try to think about how to ask if asking if everything is okay is okay, and then my phone is ringing and it's Grandma.

"Hello, may I please speak to Alexandra Eager?" she asks, the way she always does, even though I have explained one million times that a feature of personal cell phones is that you mostly always know who's going to be answering.

"Hi, Grandma," I say, and for some reason everyone else stops talking just then, so my voice sounds extra loud and I feel my cheeks and neck get hot.

"Where are you?" Grandma asks, and there's a tightness in her voice that travels through the phone, down my throat, all the way to my stomach.

"It's Tuesday," I say, and imagine everyone wondering why I just told my grandma what day it was. "Youth Council," I add. "I'll come home right after."

"Oh my goodness, of course it is," Grandma says with a little, brittle laugh. "Right there on the calendar, I see it now. Never retire, Alex. I'll see you soon, love. Bye, now."

"Bye," I say. *Never retire* is one of Grandma's favorite sayings since she retired. I don't like it, but it's better than her other favorite: *Don't get old.*

I scoot closer to PJ. She's a battery, and I need to be charged. We're already next to each other, but I want actual contact, even if it's just the sole of my shoe touching the sole of hers. Now my right sole is touching her left one, and she even presses her foot against mine a little, but she's put down the shaker egg she was cleaning and is on her phone. I can't see who she's texting. Her thumbs are moving fast, and she's frowning.

Youth Council never takes long to go from silence to chaos, and now that most of the storytime toys are clean and there's no other immediate task, we have arrived at chaos. Yesenia has her phone propped up against the wall so she can film herself doing a dance challenge, which there isn't really room enough to do, but that never bothers her; she's laughing as she dances, she is basically made of rubber and energy, and we all know she can't get through a meeting without some kind of movement. Enrique and Faisal are arguing about what the best weapon is in the game everyone but me is obsessed with currently. Linh's the only one listening to Alonso. He's talking softly, almost whispering.

"Hey, everybody, we need to focus right now!" says Linh. "Alonso, can you say all that again please? Some people weren't listening."

"Thanks, Linh," says Alonso, "but we're just about out of time. If you all could start putting the toys back in the bin and cleaning up your wrappers?"

"But you were saying—" Linh says, and Alonso cuts her off.

"Yes, and we'll definitely talk more, just not this exact minute. Can we agree that some things need more time to discuss?"

"What needs more time?" asks Yesenia while lunging to grab all the granola bar wrappers within reach of her long thin arms.

"You'd know if you'd been paying attention," says Linh.

TWO

BY THE TIME WE HAD EVERYTHING CLEANED up after Youth Council, Kyla was parked outside the library and didn't offer to drive me home, so I guess whatever PJ's stuff is probably takes a while to get to.

I don't mind walking, although it's always nice to get a ride that somewhat prolongs my time with PJ. When I walk, it takes like twenty minutes, or half an hour if I'm dawdling, as Grandma would say. First I go by U Pull U Save Auto Recycling. They have big barky dogs that used to scare me, until one time I was walking with Yesenia and she told me I should think of them as saying "Hey! Hey! Person! Person!" and that they were just doing their job. Then there's Mill Creek Nursery, where Yesenia's mom works, and then the rest of the way it's mostly small houses set back a ways from the road, with big trees in the yard and sometimes flower and vegetable gardens, too, and also the kind of stuff ("junk" according to Grandma) that people put in their gardens, like gnomes, and pinwheels that spin in the breeze, and those signs that are supposed to look like bent-over fat gardening ladies wearing flowered underwear, but remind me more of mushrooms.

One house has a Loch Ness monster made from cut-up half-buried tires. And there's this other house, about halfway between the library and home, where they have a jasmine-covered fence, and when I smell the jasmine, it's kind of like a reset from school-and-Youth-Council time to home. But today I don't notice the jasmine or anything else because I'm worrying about what PJ's stuff is. What if she's really sick and Kyla's taking her to a special doctor? She seems fine, but I know from hearing about what happened to my grandpa that sometimes someone can seem fine and then suddenly die.

"Breakfast for dinner!" Grandma announces when I come in. "I picked up cinnamon rolls from Riley's, and I'll start the bacon now you're home." We hug.

"Sounds great!" I say. Did she get cinnamon rolls because she wanted to make up for not knowing what day it was?

"How was Youth Council?" Grandma is pulling bacon slices apart and laying them on a baking sheet. We always bake bacon—we like it crispy—and save the grease. Our kitchen is small, but big enough that I can sit on a stool at what Grandma calls "the breakfast bar" but is really just a shelf with a butcher-block top, across from the stove. The breakfast bar holds cookbooks, and it's also mostly where we eat unless we eat in front of the TV. Every so often we eat at the actual table, but something about it always feels off, maybe because there are four chairs and only two of us.

"We cleaned the storytime toys," I say.

"Good for you!" Grandma says as though cleaning toys is a big accomplishment, and it makes me happy and sad at the same time, like, I want her to be proud of me for something bigger, but I'm glad she's glad about the small thing I actually did.

She's humming as she puts the bacon in the oven. Grandma hums and sings a lot, old songs that I don't always like. But I do like her singing voice; it's warm and strong and she stays on pitch. And she always sounds sure of herself when she sings.

Breakfast for dinner is perfect. The bacon is crisp and entirely unfloppy. The cinnamon rolls are warm enough that the icing is gooey but not hot enough to burn our mouths. We take our plates to the living room, and as usual, Grandma sits in her recliner and I sit on the floor, using the coffee table as a dinner table. Also as usual, Snufkin comes out from under the couch to beg, and I give him a little bacon.

Snufkin is our cat. He's named after Snufkin in the Moomin books, because Snufkin likes to go off by himself, and you never know quite when he'll come back, but he always does. Our Snufkin is small and gray and dignified and fairly aloof but will sometimes nudge us and purr. It's almost October, so it's just starting to get chilly enough that Snufkin might sleep on my stomach tonight. That's the only other form of affection he seeks out, and probably it's not even really affection so much as him knowing that me and Grandma are heat sources.

We watch one of Grandma's mystery shows, an episode about a missing girl. "Girl," but she's a grownup, basically, and the mystery is where she is and who took her. The detective is a quiet intense lady who gets people to talk just by looking at them and saying "Tell me about that," which seems more like something a therapist would say than a detective, but it works.

"No one took that girl," Grandma says. "She took herself."

This is Grandma's specialty, solving the mystery really quickly. Even when the murderer was the detective's sidekick, which I didn't think was allowed. I've given up asking her how she always knows—she can't explain it—and instead I ask, "Why?"

Grandma sighs. "Family," she says. "Something the family wanted for her that she didn't."

And sure enough, after another twenty minutes of Detective Therapist Lady looking sternly at people and computers and finding clues, it turns out the girl is alive and well and working at an animal rescue organization instead of the family meatpacking business.

"But I don't get why she couldn't just tell them? Why did she have to disappear?"

"Well, it's TV, and if she had just told them, there'd be no story."

"But couldn't there be a story of the family learning why it was important to her to do what she wanted?"

"Less dramatic," says Grandma, scratching Snufkin's head, "and that assumes the family would listen."

I NEVER FOUND OUT FROM PJ ABOUT HOW

her stuff went, but she texted to invite me for dinner at Vince's 24 Hours on Friday, which will be our eight-day anniversary of being girlfriends, and of course I said yes and got a happy buzzing feeling. It'll be especially perfect because Friday is the night Grandma has book club, so I won't have to feel bad that she's in the house with just Snufkin. Sometimes I'll think about that in the middle of class—just, Grandma being alone—and I'll freeze up and stop being able to focus. Sometimes I'll even call her between classes, but it's hard because the halls are loud and there's only a few minutes before I have to be to the next class, so almost by the time I've said hello I have to go, and that makes it worse.

"Why are you spacier than usual?" Yesenia demands while we're at our lockers after lunch.

I look up from my phone—I've been staring at it, not calling. "Sorry, what?"

"Fasten this?" Yesenia has this one bracelet, silver-colored with a white enamel flower on a black background, and the clasp is always coming undone. She says I'm the only one who can get it to stay closed for more than a minute. I think it would stay on better if she wasn't always waving her arms around and making it jingle, but if she wasn't doing that, she wouldn't be her. She sticks out her wrist, and I clasp the bracelet.

"Thanks!" She makes it jingle, the clasp unclasps, and I fasten it again.

"I'm not spacey," I say. "I just have a lot on my mind."

"Oh right!" Yesenia says. "PJ, PJ, and wait, I forgot—PJ!"

I can't tell if she's teasing in a good way or if she's actually mad. She was the first friend we told, and she seemed happy for us but also sort of weirded out, not in a homophobic way, but just sort of confused as to why we were making it into a big thing. Yesenia doesn't have crushes, or at least she hasn't said anything about having any, so it makes sense that she wouldn't get why it was important to us.

Today PJ has swimming after school, which she has every day except Tuesday. Last year I went to watch her once, but it was boring and stressful at the same time. I could barely see her in the water, and I didn't know what I was supposed to be paying attention to, and I was also worried about people making fun of me for being there, because when you're fat and you're within, like, a hundred yards of anyone who is exercising in any way, there's always someone who feels like it's their job to ask why you're not doing it, too.

"Not just PJ," I say, blushing.

THREE

VINCE'S 24 HOURS (WE ALWAYS SAY IT LIKE 24 Hours is part of the name even though technically it's just describing when it's open) has been around since Grandma was a kid, on the square right next to Faith's Fashions and Formal. It's always had a candy section and a soda fountain and diner-type food. But the best thing about Vince's 24 Hours is the secret menu, which isn't that secret really, but you do have to know that it exists, which PJ and I do, obviously. The secret menu has potstickers and shu mai and har gow and xiao long bao and baozi—just lots of amazing Chinese dumplings in different shapes and sizes and flavors.

First I think I should wear my anniversary outfit all day, but then I worry it will get messed up, so I decide that I'll change after school. Then I worry that changing will make it too big a deal. But PJ invited me on this date in the first place, so it's okay for it to be a big deal, and in fact it's polite to dress up, or maybe not exactly dress *up*, which usually means formal and uncomfortable, but to dress *nice*, like I'm happy to be going out for dinner with my girlfriend.

There are two kinds of outfits I feel mostly okay in:

kind-of-close-fitting shirts and loose pants, and kind-of-close-fitting pants and loose shirts. And I like scarves and bandannas and suspenders and sometimes buttons and pins, but the problem with buttons and pins is the tiny holes they leave in fabric and also that they say both too much and not enough, like, say you have a pin with a picture of a unicorn, and to you it might just symbolize the friend who gave it to you (Yesenia), but someone looking at it might think it means you like all unicorns, or even all fantasy-type creatures. So mostly I just stick buttons and pins onto my bulletin board at home.

What I end up wearing:

- navy-blue-and-white striped shirt (loose)
- jeans (kind-of-close-fitting)
- gray motorcycle vest made of sweatshirt material (also loose)
- rainbow high-top sneakers (the only rainbow article of clothing I own)

Buying the rainbow sneakers was a little awkward because I wasn't sure if Grandma would be okay with getting them for me. She looked at the sneakers like they already smelled bad and said, "A bit garish," and I said, "They'll go with everything because they have all the colors!" and she said, "As long as you don't plan on wearing them to church," which I think she would've said about any sneakers, not just rainbow ones. Also, we don't even go to church that often, and when we do, not everyone there is super dressed up anyway, but I think sometimes when Grandma has these kinds of opinions they're based more in how things were a long time ago than how they are now, but the times I've tried to point this out, it has not gone well.

***

GRANDMA DROPPED ME OFF AT VINCE'S 24 Hours a little early on the way to book club, so I went to the candy section and picked out some cordials for me and PJ to share. We like cordials because anything that has more than one texture is inherently more interesting, and cordials have, like, regular chocolate-bar-type chocolate on the outside but liquidy centers. Also, they're flavored with liqueurs, which feels sort of daring. Although if you wanted to get drunk from cordials, you'd get sick from sugar way before. I get some rum, some crème de menthe, and some cherry, carefully scooping each flavor into its own red-and-white striped bag and labeling the bags, like getting bulk spices at Better Bites only more exciting.

I'm just paying when PJ walks in, making the little bell jingle, which is so much nicer than the stores that use the electronic kind that sounds like an alarm, like right away they want you to know they're watching you.

"You got cordials! I was going to!"

I grin and hold up the bags. "Beat you to it. You could get different flavors?"

PJ examines them. "You got the best ones. Maybe I'll get some of the rosewater kind for my moms."

I make a face.

"I know," she says. "They totally taste like soap. But they really love them for some reason."

Should I get some for Grandma? If I do, I won't have enough money to pay for my part of dinner, though. I'll save some for her of the kinds I just got.

PJ pays for the weird rosewater candy, and then we go stand over by the WELCOME PLEASE WAIT HERE TO BE SEATED sign to do what the sign says. There are a few people ahead of us, but soon we're in one of the worn wooden booths, looking at the names carved and drawn on the table. At some point the owners of Vince's 24 Hours must have given up on trying to stop people from doing things to the tables—and that point was definitely way before I was born, which I know because sometimes people put a date next to their names.

PJ takes a silver metallic Sharpie out of her hoodie and writes our initials very small in a corner: *PJS + AJE*. Then she hands it to me, and I add an even tinier heart underneath the plus sign—if I drew it around our initials, the shape might come out wrong. As is, my hand shakes a little, but the heart still looks like a heart, maybe a little lopsided but basically okay. I think about other people seeing our initials, and it makes me nervous but also happy.

"Happy anniversary!" says PJ, and reaches across the table for my hand. I take hers and squeeze it, and then because somehow I can't just sit still holding hands with her, I shift my grip and say, "One, two, three, four! Let's have a thumb war!" PJ's thumb is longer than mine, but mine is very flexible, and I manage to squish her thumb down for the three seconds that mean I win, and that's when the waitress comes up, so I let go.

We each order a Dumpling Flight, which means they bring you one of every kind they have. And also tea, which I don't always like but is excellent here. It tastes green, in the best way.

"Thank you for thinking of doing this," I say once the waitress is gone.

She smiles and looks down at the table and runs her hand through her hair, which is messily perfect, the longish part in the front sort of standing up in a swoopy way, the back freshly buzzed.

"I love that they call it a flight," I go on. "It makes me picture all the dumplings up in the sky like clouds."

"Or in formation like geese," says PJ.

"Yes! Which one would be the lead?"

"Har gow," PJ says like she's stating an obvious fact.

"Because it's your favorite," I say, overly pleased to know.

"And yours is potstickers." It's even nicer that she knows mine.

Then the flights come, with all the sauces, chili and mustard and black bean garlic and plum, and for a while we don't talk, just enjoy.

"So what was your stuff you had to do, the other day?" I finally ask.

PJ dips her index finger into the dish where she's mixed a lot of chili sauce with a little plum, licks it off, then says, "For swimming. You know how the pools here aren't really big enough? We were looking at one I could maybe use instead for training, but it's far, so I don't know."

"How far? Would you have to, like, move?" We've only been girlfriends for eight days.

"I don't know. I hope not. Can I have a cherry cordial?"

"Of course," I say, and hand her the bag. She gets out a cordial, dips it in the chili and plum sauce, pops the cordial in her mouth.

"So good! You have to try it!" she says, muffled with her mouth full of chili-plum-cherry-cordial, extending the bag in one hand, sauce dish in the other.

I laugh and dip a cordial of my own into the sauce, and it's good, so good like PJ just said it would be, but also it burns.

SATURDAY IS GROCERY DAY, WHICH MEANS

Walmart even though Grandma doesn't like them. She says they drove the old grocery, which was called Best Foods, out of business. Better Bites Natural Grocers is still around, but what they mostly have is spices that we don't usually need, vitamins and supplements that Grandma says are just a racket, and fancy-ish organic produce that Grandma says is too spendy. I think it's funny that there used to be both Best Foods and Better Bites. Like, was Better Bites supposed to be better than Best?

Anyway, Grandma thinks it's ridiculous that Walmart sells clothes and house stuff and so many other things that are not food. "Why would you want a shirt from the grocery?" she asks, as though she thinks the shirts must be stored next to something gross.

There aren't many other places to get clothes in Failin, to be honest. There's Bend the Trend Resale next to Grumpy Grandpa Pizza out at the strip mall, but Grandma doesn't like buying used; she thinks the clothes will be dirty or have bugs or something; I don't really get it. And there's Faith's Fashions and Formal, but it's too expensive and also because the one time we did come in, the lady looked me up and down and said, "Sweetheart, we have some nice scarves right over there I think you'll really like," when what we were looking for was pants, and it's not like there weren't pants there that would have fit me, they had some that had stretch, but it was like she didn't even want me trying them on.

"I guess it's supposed to be convenient?" I say to Grandma about grocery shirts, and she sniffs.

"Too convenient."

We're in line for the one actual cashier (Grandma also doesn't like self-checkout stations) when someone says, "Kathy! How are you?"

It's the woman behind us, who looks a little younger than Grandma. Maybe she's a library person? Then I think I'm stereotyping because of her glasses, but the woman goes on: "Keeping busy? That can't be your little Alex! Hello!" she says to me.

"Um, sorry, but I don't know who you are?" I confess. The woman smiles as though I've said something funny.

"Oh, of course you wouldn't remember me—but I worked right near your grandma, so I saw a lot of pictures of you!"

I've been trying to kind of keep an eye on Grandma the whole time the woman's been talking to us, but at the same time also keep looking at the woman to be polite. As soon as she says she worked near her, something in Grandma's face changes and she says, "Nice to see you! How's Maisie?"

"She's getting up there, but she's still a big goofball!"

I decide Maisie is probably a dog.

"Glad to hear it!" says Grandma, and then it's time to pay for the groceries and go.

"I just can't come up with that woman's name for the life of me," says Grandma as I put the last bag into the trunk. I get in, shut the door, buckle my seat belt. Grandma pulls cautiously out of the parking space and gets on the road.

"You remembered her dog," I say after a while, and Grandma laughs and says, "Oh my, yes, she'd talk your ear off about the dog. Shepherd mix, one blue eye and one green. Brought her in a few times. A sweet dog, very calm. She did periodicals ordering—Ann! Ann Kehrer, that's it. Thank goodness."

While Grandma's been saying all this she's been driving, but not going the way to our house.

"Is there another errand we need to run?" I ask while we're at a stop sign.

"My goodness, I was taking us to the library," Grandma says. "Seeing Ann Kehrer must have put it in my head. Ha! No, we'd best get home before things start to melt."

FOUR

ON TUESDAY WHEN WE GOT TO THE LIBRARY for Youth Council, the Creeper was occupied with a man who was yelling about a government conspiracy while waving around what looked like a big juice box but was actually wine. The Creeper was talking to him very softly and calmly, and I was thinking that maybe he wasn't totally awful at his job, and then the yelling man yelled that the Creeper couldn't tell him what to do and called him a homophobic slur, and the Creeper slowly steered him outside.

I wonder how often the Creeper gets yelled at and if different angry people use different awful words.

"They just kicked out another drunk guy," Enrique announces when he comes in a few minutes after me and PJ. Yesenia and Faisal were already there when we got there. "These guys are so dumb," Enrique goes on. "Like, why would you think you could just hang out and get wasted in the library?" he asks the room.

"People who are having a rough time in their lives don't always have great judgment," says Alonso. "You don't know what all might be going on with someone unless you know them, okay? Sometimes not even then." He sounds tired and maybe even angry, and his eyes look kind of red and he's got dark circles, which he doesn't usually have. Everybody goes quiet. I get up and start passing out the snacks—knockoff Oreos and little bags of chips.

"What are we doing today?" asks Yesenia, and Faisal says, "You have to tell everybody about the thing from last week; you said you'd know more today."

Alonso says, "Do you still want to do the costume and candy party for the littles?"

"Definitely!" says Yesenia. For the past couple of Halloweens we've hosted a party for small kids where we also get to dress up. It's pretty fun.

"Well, you need to plan that out some more. Do you want to have stations again?"

We spend a while figuring out what to do. We'll have a drawing and collage station, because sometimes the littles want to make art of their characters, and we'll do a photo booth, which will be the old puppet stage. Also face painting because PJ's really good at it, and giving out candy because obviously. We want to give out prizes for the best costumes, but Alonso reminds us there's no prize budget.

"There might be no budget for literally anything," says Faisal, "like, not even for the library to stay open. Right?" He looks at Alonso.

Alonso cracks his neck and it's loud, and I wonder if it hurt. "You all might already know there's an election coming up.

Depending on how it goes, there might be some new city council members," he says.

"What does that have to do with the library budget exactly?" I feel like I should already know, so I feel bad about asking, but it seems important to understand.

"Well, the city is where we get our funding from, and city council members are the people who vote on Failin's budget. So if some new council members get elected, and if those new council members turn out to have some different priorities for spending the city's money, well, then there's a possibility—but I don't want you all getting caught up in speculating."

"How dumb would people have to be to not give money to a library?" Enrique asks.

"We can campaign for city council to support FPL!" says PJ. "My mama Kyla has done community organizing, she could help—we could work on messaging at our meetings!"

"Thanks for that idea," says Alonso, "but you can't do anything like that at these meetings. We can provide information, but library staff can't encourage anyone to vote one way or the other on anything."

"That's so dumb!" says Enrique.

"You think everything is dumb," I say.

"Isn't there a group that helps with stuff like this? The ones who randomly gave us thirty bucks that one time just for, like, existing?" Linh asks.

"Oh yeah, I remember, we got Grumpy Grandpa's!" Yesenia says. "It was really good."

"Friends of the Library," says Alonso. "They . . . haven't been real active lately. But! What you choose to do on your own time, that you don't talk to me about, is your business. And speaking of time, we're out of it for today."

YOU'D THINK WE MIGHT HAVE ALL STUCK

around after the meeting to talk more about what Alonso told us. But Yesenia does shelving for extra service hours, and Enrique's dad is always right on time to pick him up, and Faisal and Linh do tutoring, and Grandma worries if I'm not home, and Rachel is waiting for PJ just after the meeting, too. And not all of us even see each other much between meetings, and we don't have a group text, because not all of us have phones.

That evening I ask Grandma about the election and city council and the library, and she says some people don't want to pay for anything they don't see the point of, especially if it gets talked about as "you could have police and firefighters, or you could have books." So I ask her about Friends of the Library and if they'll do anything, and she says they never really got their act together after Linda stopped running it. I ask when Linda stopped running it, and it was before I was born.

After that, to be honest, I stop thinking about it, because I'm thinking about Friday, when a) there's no school, and b) I'm going to PJ's for the first sleepover since we've been girlfriends. We won't get to spend the entire day together because she has swimming, of course—the coach I guess sees school being closed as a reason to have an even longer practice than usual—but I'll meet her when she's done, and maybe we'll go to Vince's 24 Hours again since she's always hungry after practice, or maybe somewhere else in our very tiny "downtown."

Usually it stresses me out a little when I don't know exactly what's going to happen, because I like to be just generally prepared. But as cheesy as it sounds, not knowing exactly what we're going to do is okay, because whatever it is, I know I'll be with her.

PJ's team gets to use the high school pool when schools are closed. It's bigger than the one we have at Failin Middle, but I guess still not big enough or not available at the right times or otherwise somehow defective. She hasn't brought up the far-away pool again, though, so I haven't, either.

When I meet her at the bus bench outside the high school, she has her giant military surplus backpack that used to be Rachel's. I also have a backpack, because sleepover, but it's smaller. "You're very chloriney," I tell her as we hug.

"Yeah, they chlorinate, like, aggressively," she says.

"Are you okay? Do you need to shower again, or—" I blush. PJ grins.

"I'm good," she says. "I mean, as long as it doesn't bother you."

"Oh no, not at all! Just, if, I don't know, like, your skin was feeling too dry, or—" Apparently I can't finish a sentence that involves PJ's body.

She's fully giggling. "It's okay, I moisturized," she says, dragging out *moisturized*.

"Well, as long as your skin is moist enough," I'm barely able to say, because I'm laughing too hard and so is she—we're doubled over, writhing around on the bus bench as though nothing has ever been as funny as any variation on the word *moist*.

The bus pulls up as we're starting to recover; it's not too crowded, and we get our favorite spot at the back to ourselves.

PJ retrieves an energy bar from somewhere in the giant backpack. "Let's go to Faithful Angus and look at weird old things," she says as she unwraps it.

"Sure!"

Faithful Angus Antique Mall is sort of set off by itself on the outskirts, a word that makes me picture actual skirts in multiple layers. PJ looks up the stop for it, and we ride in silence for a while, every so often showing each other a funny picture or video on our phones. PJ gets a text from Rachel asking about my food restrictions—she can never remember that I don't really have any, or maybe she thinks I might get some suddenly? PJ says she's just used to asking because they have lots of friends who don't or can't eat various things. It's nice that she asks. By the time we get to the stop, there are only two other people on the bus, and one of them, a woman using a wheelchair who has the best tiny dachshund on her lap, is getting off, too, so we wait for the ramp to descend and then for the woman and her dachshund; then we clamber down the ramp ourselves.

One great thing about the antique mall is that despite how small Failin is overall, Faithful Angus is the opposite of a Cool Teen Destination, so there's very little risk of seeing anyone we know and don't want to see. One not-so-great thing about the antique mall is that most of the people who work there tense up when we get close to anything and are constantly telling us to be careful, as though just by being young we are the natural enemies of antiques.

There are some things we basically always see at Faithful Angus: overly fancy china, creepy dolls, rusty implements that maybe once had some farming-related function but are now supposed to be decor, and big piles of old photos.

We start looking through the old-photo piles. I like finding pictures of pets. "There's no way any of those animals are around anymore, so it's kind of morbid," says PJ, and I say that's likely true of the people, too. We decide that in this situation being morbid is totally acceptable and maybe even good, because we're looking at people and pets that might not otherwise be getting remembered or thought about by anyone. Even though sometimes we're also making fun of their outfits and hair or how the photos are blurry or overexposed or both. Or when there's a giant finger covering up part of the picture.

"Maybe it was on purpose," PJ says after we find the third one where that's happening. One's at a beach, and the finger blocks the sun. One's at a little-kid birthday party, the finger covering a kid's face. One's at Christmas, with the finger on top of the tree instead of a star. "Yeah," I say, "maybe there was a whole trend of putting fingers in photos and we're just too young to know about it."

"Like how now they have, what's the thing where there's like a name across it so you can't just copy it?"

"Yeah I think it's called a watermark? I don't know why, though."

It's not the same thing, but it makes me think of how where

Mill Creek runs close to town, there's a retaining wall along the banks, and Grandma always comments on the waterline. "Looking rather high," she'll say, "basements will be flooding." And our basement does tend to flood, so we don't keep much down there.

"Oof, yuck, why's this here?" PJ asks. "This shouldn't even exist, let alone be getting sold."

She beckons me closer—we've been standing on opposite sides of the table where the photo piles are stacked—and points, like what she's been looking at might contaminate us if we touch it.

I recognize the stage at the Grange Hall, a place I've been a million times. The Failin Fall Festival happens there, and Christmas-tree lighting, and weddings and concerts and graduations.

And at least one time, I now know from the worn black-and-white photo, the Ku Klux Klan met there.

The white men sitting on the Grange stage are all wearing the white robes and ridiculous conical hats I've seen in history textbooks and TV and movies. But they aren't hiding their faces behind masks, the way I thought they always did. They're all grinning, like it was a Klan class photo. Which I guess in a way maybe it was.

"We should tear it up," says PJ, reaching for it.

I stop her hand with mine. "No we shouldn't!"

"What, you don't want to get in trouble?" She reaches for it again; I block her hand again.

She's right that I don't want to get in trouble. I never want to get in trouble.

But that's not why. I'm thinking about the old photos Grandma's kept, and how they're almost the only way I know anything about my grandpa and my mom. And a photo doesn't tell a whole story, but it does do something.

"No," I say. "Because—because it's like evidence." I'm thinking of Grandma's mystery shows again, and I go on: "Like, this actually happened. Tearing it up would just make it easier for people to pretend it didn't."

"Oof," PJ says.

We stare at the grinning Klan men a while longer. The photo is too old to have my grandpa in it, but what about my grandpa's dad, my great-grandfather? Was he one of them? I really hope not. He was a farmer, and Grandma says he drank, and that's all I know. I look harder at the faces. I don't think any of them are him, but also they kind of all look like they could be?

"Okay, so you definitely changed my mind about this, but I don't want to look at it anymore. Can we hide it and go back to looking for evidence that people in the past loved their pets?" PJ asks.

I nod, and she shoves the KKK photo between the pages of a 1928 Failin High yearbook.

Then I find a photo without a finger that's mostly of a barn but also of a Dalmatian. The Dalmatian is squinting into the sun and the barn door is open, and you can see that there are things inside, but the light isn't strong enough to see what they are, and you can't do the thing you can do with photos on screens where you can zoom in, so I'll never know what was in there, and realistically it probably wasn't very interesting. But I like the dog's expression and the small mystery and also it only costs a dollar.

"Look," says PJ. "Look at this one!" She's cradling the photo between her hands like she's showing me a kitten.

The photo is of two women, both with long hair piled on top of their heads, wearing high-necked dresses with puffy sleeves. It's even older than the KKK class photo, sepia-toned with stiff backing. I think mostly people didn't smile in pictures way back then, but these two are smiling, and also they're looking at each other instead of the camera. "They're like us if we'd been alive back then," PJ says. "I'm getting it."

Part of me wonders if PJ thinks they look like a past version of us because one of them is much bigger than the other, and I get sad and self-conscious even though that is objectively true about us, and then she says, "It's how they're looking at each other," and smiles the same smile as the women.

We have to pay for our photos right away, because if we carry them around while we look at stuff in other stalls, the staff will think we're trying to steal them. But when the man at the counter rings us up, he doesn't look suspicious of us like they usually do. He even says "Good eye!" to PJ and "Nice shoes!" to me. I say, "They're extremely rainbow!" which is dumb but also somehow hilarious, and PJ and I go into another one of the unstoppable laughing flailing fits that make people think we're going to break things, and, in fact, two glass giraffes on a nearby shelf are seriously wobbling, so I grab her arm and drag us away from the counter before they fall.

PJ AND RACHEL AND KYLA'S HOUSE IS LIT-

tle, but their yard is pretty big. There's the barkless tree where we officially became girlfriends, of course, and Kyla's serious about gardening, so she also always has a lot of different stuff growing, flowers and herbs and vegetables, and projects that she's in the middle of, like clearing out blackberry bushes (we helped with that once; it was not fun), or harvesting whatever's ripe, which right now is apples. Rachel says they should be getting a big break on rent for all the work Kyla does. Kyla says she likes doing it, and it's cheaper than therapy.

We each pick an apple and walk to the back door, the only door anyone uses. Before we're close enough for PJ to unlock it, we hear Rachel, very loud: "—denying our kid opportunities because of your own selfishness!"

Kyla says something we can't hear—she's always quieter—and then Rachel's yelling again: "Your family barely wants to admit I exist, so forgive me if I'm not devastated at the prospect of being farther from them! Maybe you don't remember how long we'd been together before your mom deigned to even put my name in her holiday letter, but I do, and, Kyla, it was five years."

It's not the first time I've overheard them argue. They have a kind of constant squabbly energy that seems to just be how they are with each other—but always before, I've had the feeling they were on the same side. This doesn't feel like that, and I don't think it's just because we can only hear Rachel's voice. I'd reach out for PJ, but I can't even look at her; I'm looking, ridiculously, at the apple I'm holding, red-pink-yellowish, with a bruise I didn't see when I picked it, and suddenly I'm wondering if there's a worm inside.

The back door opens onto the utility room—washer, dryer, gardening tools. The air's a little steamy, full of fabric softener.

Kyla's ironing a white button-down shirt within an inch of its life, as Grandma would say. She looks up, but before she can say or do anything, Rachel's across the room and hugging us both, backpacks and all.

"Welcome!" Rachel and Kyla are usually happy to see me, and I'm happy to see them, too, but this greeting from Rachel is a little extreme. "You're squishing us," PJ says, and Rachel lets go.

The dryer is loudly thudding with a heavy unbalanced load, which I know because that happens with ours sometimes, too.

Kyla shakes out the shirt she was ironing, puts it on a hanger, and hangs it on the line strung across the room. "Hi, girls."

"Are you hungry?" Rachel asks abruptly. "I'm hungry. Let's make something. No, let's order something. I can't face combining ingredients. Pizza? You eat pizza, right, Alex?" Rachel knows I eat pizza. Or at least she usually knows I eat pizza.

"She does," says Kyla. "I don't mind cooking. Think we have some frozen crusts, turkey pepperoni, zucchini, tomatoes, basil, there's fresh mozzarella from the farmer's market the other day . . ." She keeps softly naming ingredients as she walks toward the kitchen. Just before she gets all the way out of the utility room, she turns. "Babe, can I put you and the girls in charge of the salad?"

The dryer stops shaking, and Kyla adds, "But, PJ, first I need you to fold the laundry and put it away."

Rachel says, "So we're just done talking about this?"

PJ says, "Why do I need to do it now? Alex is here."

Kyla says, "You know why. It's one of your jobs, and if it doesn't get folded right away, everything wrinkles—"

"I don't care if it wrinkles!" PJ yells.

"Well, I do," Kyla says, voice getting quieter.

I blurt out, "PJ, let's just do it—I can help."

Rachel bangs on the lid of the dryer. "Fine!"

She follows Kyla out of the utility room.

Neither PJ or me have taken our backpacks off. I'm still holding the apple, and at some point I must have pressed my thumb into its bruise without noticing. Now my thumb is sticky, and a faint rotting-apple scent combines with the fabric softener. I put the apple in the wastebasket next to the dryer, then worry that I should have put it in compost instead, but there's not a compost bin in here. I put my sticky thumb in my mouth, just for a second, to get it unsticky, and wish I was still little enough to get away with keeping it there.

PJ and I don't talk while we're folding. It's a load of sheets and towels and pillowcases, and I'm glad it's not, like, underwear. When everything's stacked on top of the dryer, PJ says, "Wait here a minute."

She goes after her moms. I take my backpack off finally and sit on the floor. It's concrete and cold but somehow comforting in how solid it is. I try not to think about anything, which doesn't work. After a while I get up and refold the laundry, like somehow if it's really well folded that will make everything okay.

Rachel and PJ come back together, and Rachel says, "We decided we need to watch a super-gay movie! How does that sound, Alex?"

"Sure," I say, and feel my face heat up in the way I hate. It's not that I don't want to watch a super-gay movie, but I don't see any way for it not to be awkward to watch whatever it is with PJ's moms. And I still want to know about PJ's opportunities, except that also I don't. We all go into the kitchen, where Kyla's already assembled the pizzas. She's gotten out a salad bag, so all we have to do is open it, dump it into the big wooden bowl that she's also gotten out, and mix in the sesame seeds, dried cranberries, and dressing.

Just as I've ripped open the dressing packet, PJ says, "Ugh, we don't ever use that dressing—it's gross; we make our own!" She tries to grab the packet out of my hand, and the dressing squirts everywhere: our hands, the salad, the wall, her shirt. PJ makes this half-scream, half-growl sound: I've ruined the salad, and probably the stain won't come out from where the dressing splotched onto PJ's shirt, and Rachel, suddenly, is laughing so hard!

"Kiddo!" she gasps out. "Oh, kiddo, your face right now! It's okay, it's totally okay. PJ, how was your lovely Alex supposed to know that we don't use everything in the salad kit? Just, here"—she holds out her hand for the crumpled dressing packet—"I'll take that, and you two get yourselves settled." She tosses the packet across the kitchen into the wastebasket in a perfect arc.

PJ's stomping out of the kitchen, so I follow her.

The second we get into PJ's room, she yanks her shirt over her head and I almost take mine off, too, although that is not a step we have taken or even discussed. But then I remember the salad-dressing stain and realize she's just changing into something clean, and I go back to what I was actually doing, which was climbing the little ladder to put my backpack on the top bunk. There isn't much room because mostly the top bunk has all the stuffed animals PJ thinks would prefer a higher vantage point: the unicorn, obviously, and the rainbow manatee and the sloth, whose sleepy smile I always find soothing.

My favorite of PJ's stuffed animals is the one I made her: a mole, because we both like their sensitive noses and clever digging paws. First PJ called him Mole in the Ground, after Grandma's favorite folk song. She taught it to us a long time ago, and we like it a lot, too. It's honestly a deeply weird song, and I've found lots of verses and versions online: about nine-dollar shawls and lizards in the spring and railroad men who'll drink your blood like wine. Only a few lines are actually about wishing to be a mole in the ground, but that's where the title comes from. Then we realized that given that name, Mole should technically *be* in the ground, but we didn't want to put him there, so we agreed to slightly change it to Mole *of* the Ground, like Toad of Toad Hall or Anne of Green Gables or Baggins of the Shire, so it would honor where he came from. I mean, he *actually* came from fabric scraps and stuffing and a needle and thread and a little of my blood from when I stabbed myself while I was sewing him, but for our purposes, he came from the ground. Anyway, Mole of the Ground is still on her pillow, and that makes me feel a little better.

WE END UP WATCHING A BUNCH OF EPIsodes of a cartoon which is, in fact, super gay, and also very wholesome. Kyla falls asleep and is snoring until Rachel shakes her and they go up to bed.

The TV's asking if we want to continue watching. PJ and I

have been sitting on the floor, leaning against their old brown squooshy couch. The floor is concrete, like in the utility room, but has a fluffy rug over it, so it's pretty comfortable, but it's getting chilly.

The glow of the screen on PJ's face is the only light in the room.

What's different about this fight between her moms? I want to ask. I don't. After a while I say, "It's pretty cold down here, right? You want to go up?" She nods.

When we're back in her room, she says, "I don't think we should, you know, I mean, I'm not really, I can't really—"

"Of course!" I interrupt, so PJ doesn't have to keep explaining how she doesn't want to touch me. I wish she were the kind of person who wants more physical affection when something bad happens, not less, and then I'm mad at myself for being needy when I know that her moms, like, seriously fighting is worse than me just feeling bad that our first sleepover as girlfriends got ruined.

Well, okay, not *ruined* ruined. It's not like she's upset at me, which would be the worst thing. And also if she had wanted to hug and kiss, or anything else, would I even have been able to handle it?

I mean, I know I want to, or it feels like I want to, anyway, which is maybe the same thing, feeling and wanting?

But now that I know we're not going to do . . . things, a part of me, the part that wasn't sure what to do or what would be too much or how I would even know, is a tiny tiny tiny bit relieved.

I climb up to the top bunk where my backpack is and dig

into it for what I brought to sleep in: a T-shirt from last summer when we did tie-dye in Youth Council. It comes down past my knees, and it's a disastrous mix of orange, yellow, pink, and green that should definitely not all be on the same piece of clothing. I'd never wear it in front of anyone but PJ, but I do like that it's giant, so I can do the thing I'm doing now: put my head into the neck hole and let the rest of it drape around me while I wiggle out of the shirt and bra and pants I was wearing, keeping my underwear on. Then I tuck my backpack between the pillow and the wall. I like to keep it close by in case I suddenly need something out of it, like Kleenex or a tampon.

And while I've been doing that, PJ has put on her own pajamas and gone down the hall to brush her teeth, which I should do, too, but also I don't want to get out of the bunk now that I'm in it, so I don't.

When she comes back from brushing her teeth, I think about pretending to be asleep, because maybe that would be easier than talking? But also I want to do something to make her feel better, so I say, "I think you need the sloth," and hand it down to her, and she says thanks.

I kind of want to ask her for Mole of the Ground, because maybe if I were holding him he could help me sort of burrow away from feelings I don't want to feel, but also I don't want to ask PJ for anything, because I shouldn't need anything. So I hold the rainbow manatee instead, and after a while PJ gets on the floor to do push-ups.

I stop counting after forty-seven.

IN THE MORNING PJ SAYS, "I WISH YOU didn't have to go home," and I say, "I wish I didn't, either." But home is actually where I want to be. There are too many emotions happening at her house; the air is thick, it's hard to breathe.

When we get to my house, PJ hugs me so hard I imagine I can feel how every one of those push-ups last night made her stronger, and I decide not to mind that she did them, because I know she needs her strength.

I've never been more grateful for Grandma's fervent belief in the importance of Getting Rest and her associated—and accurate—belief that after any sleepover I will not have gotten enough of it. So after she thanks Rachel for hosting me—I thank her, too—she tells me to go take a nap, which means I don't need to have any conversation about whether I had a good time or what we did or anything else. Snufkin even gets on me and purrs, but I can't sleep; I stare at the ceiling and sort of drift. It would be daydreaming if what was going through my head were at all pleasant. But my brain's highest priority is to rehearse bad things that could happen. Failing the math test Monday. Showing up to the library and finding the doors padlocked. Hurting myself in gym and everyone thinking I did it on purpose to get out of exercise. PJ's moms divorcing.

Bing. Bing. Bing. Bing.

I can't make the chime stop, and that's when I realize I must have managed to slip into a kind of sleep after all and fumble for my phone to see PJ's texts.

> they're still fighting. mom keeps getting louder and mama gets quieter and i hate it unbelievably.

> ugh. i'm sorry.

> . . . what are they fighting about?

> . . .

> just stuff. i'm hiding.

> practice is soon though so that's good.

> . . .

> yeah that sounds good.

I send a swimmer emoji and a heart, and then I'm awake enough to notice what time it is, and so I text:

> yikes it's so late i have to homework.

> have a good practice.

Then I send a swimming penguin gif, then more hearts. It doesn't feel like enough.

FIVE

ON THURSDAY, AFTER I DIDN'T FAIL THE math test but didn't do great on it, either, and after PJ didn't say anything else about her moms fighting, but then again also I didn't ask because I was afraid of what she might say, and after Grandma forgot what day it was again, after all that, I have gym with Yesenia.

It was actually in gym that Yesenia and I got to be friends in the first place, way back in elementary school. I was wearing a Totoro T-shirt, and Jason Kruse asked, "Is that you? It looks like you," because of course he did because ha ha ha Totoro is big and round, and just as I was trying to think of something to say back and also trying not to cry, Yesenia said, "Wow, you don't even know that's Totoro? I feel sorry for you and your sad, Miyazaki-less life." Then she asked if I'd seen *Kiki's Delivery Service*, and we talked about movies and books for the rest of class. We were technically in the outfield for kickball, but the ball never came near us that day.

"We're doing field hockey drills today; gather round, grab a stick, find a partner!" says Mr. Stamos. I like him okay, because he doesn't seem to have total contempt for less athletically inclined people, unlike Mr. Orkutt from elementary school. Mr. Stamos mostly lets us pick our own partners, which obviously makes everything better, except if there's no one in the class you like, but since Yesenia and I have gym together, we don't have that problem.

And it's nice out—it's warm but not hot, and the fir trees that border the school grounds look especially deep green against the bright blue cloudless sky.

The field hockey sticks are a very different green, neon-highlighter green, and they're just on the ground in a pile, which makes me think of wood stacked up for a bonfire, which makes me wonder what it would be like to set the stack of sticks on fire, but I'm sure whatever they're made of would smell awful if it burned and also it would be bad for the environment.

We've never done field hockey anything before, and I'm immediately sure I'm going to be clumsy and terrible. I wait until after most of the other kids, including Yesenia, have grabbed their sticks before I cautiously bend down and take one of the last ones from the pile.

It's lighter than I thought it would be, and it feels strangely not-bad in my hands. There's tape on it that makes it easier to hold, and holding it gives me a kind of calm focus—very different from holding a baseball bat, for example; all I can think about when I'm at bat is how much my butt sticks out, how I'm scared the ball will hit me, how even if it doesn't, my swing will be wild. I'm not exactly sure where my hands are supposed to be on the field hockey stick, but just the fact that I don't have to raise it up at some weird angle makes me grateful.

Mr. Stamos gives each set of partners a ball and tells us to space ourselves out and warm up by just hitting the ball back and forth.

It's satisfying to thwock the ball to Yesenia, and when she sends it back to me and I succeed in stopping it with my stick, then hit it to her again, that's even better.

After a while, Mr. Stamos tells us all to work our way across the field. So Yesenia and I are still hitting the ball back and forth to each other, but now we're doing it while we're farther apart and also both running, and staying out of the way of everyone else. And that's harder, but it doesn't stop being satisfying. I would've thought I'd be disappointed, because the running and the distance between us means Yesenia and I can't talk the whole time like we usually do. But there's something about it that's *like* talking; the back-and-forth of it, how we each move to make sure we can retrieve the ball and send it back to the other, how we're paying such close attention. It feels like a new way to be friends, and I like it.

SIX

I COULDN'T FIND ANYTHING IN THE DONATION bin to use for a costume for the Youth Council party for the littles, so I decided to see if there was something I could use in the house.

Usually I'd ask Grandma if it was okay before going through her closet and the cedar chest, but it's a book-club night and she won't be back for a while, and also, if I'm being honest, I want to snoop.

Grandma will show me an old photo sometimes, like the one where she thought my mom was me, or maybe vice versa. And there are a few stories Grandma likes to tell, like how excited my mom was when she found out she was going to have me—I mean, not me specifically, because obviously she couldn't have known who I was going to turn out to be, but a baby—or how my grandpa was such a good singer, and sometimes he'd just make up songs on the spot. But lately I've been thinking a lot about the stuff Grandma doesn't talk to me about and feeling like there might be some clues for me to find.

When I'm not thinking about the stuff PJ doesn't talk to me

about, that is. I mean, we still send each other cute animals and memes and emojis and little videos of people being funny and/or odd, we still talk about school and Youth Council, but we haven't had a date since the sleepover. And objectively I know it wasn't that long ago—it hasn't even been two entire weeks—but I keep wondering if something happened to make her not want to be girlfriends anymore. But I can't ask her, because asking would make the possibility realer. And I would've invited PJ over tonight, which wouldn't have been a date exactly but would've been *something*, but of course, of course, of course, she has swimming.

While I'm having all these thoughts, I'm kneeling in front of the cedar chest at the foot of Grandma's bed, and I haven't opened it yet, because Snufkin is sleeping on top. I gently scoop him up and put him on the bed. Which you'd think he'd like better than the hard wood of the cedar chest, but he gives a little half meow, half hiss, jumps down, and stalks away.

One time when I was at Faithful Angus with PJ, I saw a cedar chest that looked so much like this one, I thought Grandma had sold it without telling me. But when I got closer, I saw that the Faithful Angus chest had stains on top. It looked like a little kid had maybe colored on it with a red marker, and someone had tried to clean it but ended up kind of weirdly bleaching the wood without getting rid of the red. Also it had the name Cynthia engraved on it in fancy script, so it was clear it wasn't actually ours. I wondered if it was Cynthia who got the red marker stains on it, and if it was, how much trouble she got in.

Until then I hadn't really understood that more than one family could have versions of the same piece of furniture, even though it seemed super obvious once I thought about it. There are big chain stores that all sell the same things, so of course lots of people are going to have the same, like, table or bookcase or whatever. But because I knew Grandma's cedar chest was old, I didn't think there'd be others like it.

And actually, I guess even if a cedar chest started out looking exactly like all the others that were made by the same furniture maker, it would end up different because of everything that happens once someone takes it home: where they put it, what they put in it, and how well they take care of it, or don't.

We keep Christmas ornaments in ours, and I know that under the ornament box there are a couple of extra blankets, but I've never gotten any deeper into the cedar chest than that.

Until now.

Under the blankets, there's a dark blue plastic zippered garment bag. I lift it out. It's heavy. Underneath that, there's a jewelry box, which I know because *jewelry* is wood-burned on top in swirly cursive. I'm interested in the jewelry box, but I unzip the garment bag first, slowly, because sometimes old zippers stick.

I see a wide collar, red and black stripes on a gray background, a row of shiny black buttons—a shirt? But it keeps going and the fabric swells out, so it must be a dress. I think it's a kind of cotton— it's soft but feels sort of heavy in my hands, too. It doesn't look like a dress Grandma would wear. She almost never wears dresses. She likes what she calls "nice blouses" and "slacks." I try to imagine a younger version of Grandma in this dress and I can't, and that's when it hits me.

I take it all the way out of the garment bag. It's old enough that it couldn't have been new even when my mom wore it. It might be from like the eighties? I mean if it was really my mom's. It's in very good condition, no buttons missing, no rips or sweat stains under the arms. I hold it up to myself, fully prepared for it to be so much narrower than me.

But it isn't. It still doesn't seem like it could fit. I unbutton the buttons. I like that they're in the front, so you don't have to have anyone help you get into it, which is a reason I don't usually like dresses any more than Grandma does.

Very quickly I pull off my shirt. Very slowly I put on the dress.

The sleeves don't pinch my arms.

There's room in the waist, even with my pants still on. I take them off.

It still might not button.

But it does.

Grandma has always said I look a lot like my mom, even before she pointed at the picture of my mom and said it was me. But somehow I never thought that looking like my mom would also mean that my body would be like hers.

I lift my arms over my head. I twist at the waist. I twirl.

I have to keep this dress, even though it's making me cry.

Then I hear the front door open.

I get rigid—I feel it happening. Like I'm doing really well in a game of statues. Like I've just looked at Medusa and all her hissing hair-snakes. Like I'm in a heist movie trying not to trigger the bank's motion detector.

"Now where did you get to?" Grandma asks, and I'm not sure if she means me or Snufkin or someone else, but her voice makes my body unfreeze, and I step out of her room and aim myself down the hall to meet her.

"I'm right here! I found this," I somehow say. "I love it."

Grandma takes her glasses off, rubs her eyes, puts them on again.

"Yes," she says. "I wasn't sure about those horizontal stripes, but it suits you."

I go to hug her, and she rubs my back while we're hugging like she did when I was littler, and I'm glad she's not angry about the dress, but also I wish she would've said my name.

So now that I can move my body in a semi-functional human way, my mouth is no longer working.

I smooth the skirt and look at the stripes, and then I remember something that restarts my ability to speak. "Oh gosh, I left the cedar chest open—I better check." I propel my legs back to Grandma's room, and sure enough, Snufkin is inside the chest, curled up on the garment bag. I lift him out, seeing how much he's managed to shed in the few minutes he's been sitting there. I hear Grandma setting down her tote bag, then opening the refrigerator to put away the leftover casserole from book club. She'll probably come back here next, so I grab the wooden jewelry box, bundle it up with the garment bag and the clothes I was wearing before, take the whole pile to my room, and shove it under the bed.

I don't want to take the dress off, but also I do. For the first time I'm grateful for the hangers that were a rare non-outdoors-oriented present from Dad and Laura. They're pink and silky and padded, like the kind of bras I hate, and look like they're intended for an entirely different wardrobe than mine, so they're shoved all the way to one side of the closet.

But I know their poofy slipperiness is supposed to protect fabric. I unbutton the dress, step out of it carefully, drape it on one of the fancy hangers, rebutton it, put on pajamas, and go back to the living room.

"Ready for bed? I sure am," says Grandma.

She's usually tired after book club. It doesn't necessarily mean she's already forgotten about the dress. It might mean she just doesn't want to talk about it.

Again, it's not that Grandma never talks about my mom. But when she does, I always worry that at any minute she'll get too sad and I won't be able to help, so I don't ask as many questions as I want to. And sometimes she'll say something out of nowhere, like, "When you want to have children, make sure your doctor knows your family history," which, I think I was ten when she first said that? And I know my mom died from something to do with giving birth to me, but that was kind of both too much information for ten-year-old me and not enough for a hypothetical future me who hypothetically wanted to have a kid that would grow inside my actual body. Which is a hypothetical situation that is very hard for me to imagine, and besides, what I really want to know about is not how my mom died but what she was like alive.

SEVEN

> can we have another date
>
> i mean i'd like to go on another date with you if that is something you would also like

I send a gif of a begging puppy, because I feel weirdly grovel-y, like I'm apologizing even though we haven't fought.

> yes!!!
>
> not my house
>
> somewhere out in the World

> absolutely
>
> that doesn't really narrow it down though
>
> are there any not-terrible movies

> no
>
> we could see a terrible one
>
> on purpose

> just to be
>
> you know
>
> in the dark
>
> wink emoji

> challenge accepted

THE JEWELRY BOX HAS BEEN UNDER MY

bed for days now. I haven't opened it yet, and I don't know exactly why.

Maybe because I kind of feel like I stole it, even though it's technically a family object, and therefore I shouldn't feel guilty about it being in my room instead of Grandma's?

Maybe because I kind of think Grandma was hiding it from me on purpose because she thought it would upset me, even though it's more likely that she just forgot it was there?

Maybe because until I open it, there's no limit to what I can imagine might be inside? (I mean, other than the limit of whatever it is having to fit into the available space.)

I guess it's all those things at the same time, which is a lot of feelings to have about an old wooden box that might just be empty.

I also don't know why I decide the right time to open it is right before my date with PJ.

Of course I also thought about wearing my mom's dress on our date. But I haven't been brave enough to wear it outside the house.

I've had nightmares: I get a stain on it that won't come out. I rip it and it makes everyone laugh. I come home in the stained ripped ruined dress, and Grandma scolds me, using my mom's name.

Instead I hold the dress close to my face and breathe in the cedary scent from all the time it was in the chest, feel the cool, smooth, heavy cotton against my cheeks, and that somehow gives me the courage to kneel and reach under the bed and take out the box. I glance at my phone. I have an hour before I need to leave to meet PJ at Dollar Cinema. It actually costs more than a dollar, but I guess it's been open since a time when tickets did only cost a dollar, and they've just never changed the sign.

I decide to write down a list of everything in the box and take a picture of each thing, like the detectives in Grandma's shows. My bedspread is dark green and the carpet is a sort of beige, so when I take the pictures, I'll put dark-colored things on the carpet and light-colored things on the bedspread.

There are five items in the box:

1. Light blue ticket stub. It just says ADMIT ONE, so there's no way to know what it was for.
2. Dried carnation corsage, dyed bright green and gold.
3. Big white enamel pin, the kind Grandma calls a brooch, diamond shaped with a hanging-down purple teardrop.
4. Leather cord necklace with two things strung on it: a wooden medallion with the head of a bird carved on it and a shiny black oval stone with a hole in it.

When I lift the necklace out of the box, the dry leather crumbles and breaks. My eyes get wet. I wipe them and break the cord into smaller and smaller pieces, destroying instead of documenting this evidence. I put one tiny piece of dried-out leather cord in my mouth and hold it there for a while, acrid-salty on my tongue. When it gets all the way soft I swallow it, then take out the last thing.

5. A Christmas card with a big kid and a little kid in matching sweaters.

The big kid, I'm pretty sure, is my mom, maybe a little younger than I am now. But the little one, who's in her lap and who I think is a boy although you can't assume someone's gender by looking so I could be wrong—anyway, I don't know who this other kid is, but the card, it says *Merry Christmas from the Eagers*.

OUTSIDE DOLLAR CINEMA, PJ IS JUMPING

up and down in a way that reminds me of Yesenia, except less dancey and more sporty. I really want to show her the Christmas card, which I put in a ziplock and have with me in my bag, but I also really want to have a good date that does not involve any family drama, so I don't.

"Did you get the tickets already? I'll pay you back," I say, reaching for my wallet.

"I didn't," she says, "but it's okay because, surprise, we're not really going to a movie."

"Okay," I say cautiously, "what are we doing instead?"

So much for being in the dark and the wink emoji. Although it's already almost dark outside, even though the movie we were going to see was a matinee, so maybe the dark will still be a factor.

"Just come with me," she says, and takes my hand.

Inside I go somehow gooey and fluttery at once. I will go anywhere with her.

We don't talk while we're walking, but every so often she'll squeeze my hand and I'll squeeze back, still gooey-fluttery from the strong pressure of her fingers. Her hand is warmer than mine, which I like. Every so often, too, someone will look at us and smile, or look at us and wrinkle up their faces, and it takes me a while to understand that my mood keeps changing based on these strangers' facial expressions. I go from pride to fear to, eventually, irritation that I'm letting the strangers control my emotions, and if I'm going to put anyone in charge of how I feel, I want it to be PJ, so I focus again on how we're together, on this date, alone for the next couple of hours.

Then I realize where we're going. The ravine, where we used to play when we were littler. It's not far from downtown but mostly nobody goes there, or if they do, they just go to the park the ravine is next to. We haven't been down there in a long time. It started to feel babyish to go to a place where we'd had doll and stuffed animal and action figure picnics. In spring, it was the closest we could get to Violet Vale from the Anne books. In winter, if it snowed enough, we'd take our sleds. Right before we get to the park, PJ smiles and says, "You figured it out a while ago, didn't you?"

I nod, smiling back.

"We can't stay super long because we need to be back by the time the movie's over, but it's okay because I set an alarm." PJ waves her phone, then shoves it back in her hoodie pocket.

First we have to go on the swings. We're not trying to swing high; it's more like the swings are the seating in our personal living room that is also the park. We propel ourselves back and forth gently but keep our feet on the ground. After a while we yield up the swings to some actual little kids and walk down into the ravine.

"Look! Look how many red huckleberries!" says PJ, who always knows the names of plants. And she's right: There are so many huckleberry bushes all over both sides of the ravine, and some tall yellow-gold grasses I don't know the name of. They make the tiny berries and bright green leaves stand out even more as the light fades from dusk to full dark.

There are also some tents. A blue one, a green one, a tan one with a dirty orange tarp over it—and I remember the other reason we stopped coming. The park and ravine might have felt like they belonged to us, but they weren't where we lived.

I'm starting to get uncomfortable, and then I'm uncomfortable about *being* uncomfortable, because people who don't have houses or apartments are just people who don't have houses or apartments, not fairy-tale monsters or urban-legend villains. Although maybe some of them are the same people who go to the library and yell at the Creeper? That actually does feel somewhat villainous. But then I remember what Alonso said about people who are having rough times not always having great judgment. And also I don't actually know that any of them are the same people who bring their wine-juice-boxes into the library. So then I come back around to being uncomfortable again, because it feels like we're trespassing in their yard, which is the ravine.

That's when PJ wraps her arms around me, angles her face to meet mine, and kisses me, first gentle and soft, then firm and strong, like the kiss equivalent of her push-ups. Now I'm the opposite of uncomfortable. Her lip balm smears itself onto my lips, and it actually strikes me funny, because my lips were kind of dry before and this is the best possible way I can imagine to ensure they don't get chapped, except that maybe kissing itself will eventually chap them, but that would be absolutely fine. It makes me giggle a little against her mouth, which makes her pull away, so I quickly explain my whole train of thought re: preferred lip balm application, and then she laughs, too.

"You have to start using it yourself, then; you never have any."

"That's fair," I say. "Do we need to coordinate flavors?"

"There could be some pretty tasty mixes. Lemon-raspberry."

"Root beer-vanilla."

"Mint-orange."

"Yeah, I think most of the mixes will be good. As long as we don't get any of the kind that's basically just petroleum. That's gross."

"Deal," I say. "Now that's settled—"

I break off because PJ's face has changed. Is she crying? She is—what did I do wrong? Should I hug her? Would that be too much? Finally I manage to get out a single two-word question: "What's up?" It feels like the literally dumbest possible thing I could have said, but at least it doesn't seem to have made her more upset. She crouches to pick a handful of huckleberries, so I crouch, too, glad I'm not wearing the dress, and put my hands on the wood-chip-covered path, as though being more connected to the ground will somehow help.

"I don't want to tell you," PJ says, "because I don't want it to happen."

"You don't want what to happen?"

She stares at her huckleberries, then lets them drop one by one from her hand.

"I'm moving."

EIGHT

SOME THINGS I DIDN'T DO WHEN I GOT HOME:

- my homework
- say anything to Grandma about how the girl she still thinks is just my best friend, because I haven't figured out how to tell her that PJ's my girlfriend, is moving
- cry; it's like the tears were stuck somewhere behind my eyes; they made my head hurt and feel like it was the wrong size, but they wouldn't come
- eat anything

Some things I did:

- opened the refrigerator and stared into it
- fed Snufkin; he sniffed the food, then walked away
- opened and closed every kitchen cabinet until Grandma told me from the living room to stop banging around in there
- opened the kitchen cabinet door again where we keep

the drinking glasses—why do we call them that; what else would they be for besides drinking?—and also Grandma's prescriptions

I've never paid much attention to Grandma's prescriptions, except that aesthetically I like the blue bottles more than the brown ones. Now I look at them, and my wrong-sized head can't let go of how I don't know what any of them are for, all the tiny-print directions and warnings. I take pictures of each one with my phone so I can look them all up. But when I open my computer, because it's easier to do research with a bigger screen, what I do instead is find out how many miles away Portland is. Then I finally do cry, but my head doesn't feel any better.

NINE

I SOMEHOW FORGOT THAT TODAY ISN'T just a Youth Council meeting; it's the party for the littles, and I was supposed to dress up. Everyone else has something, even if it's just cat ears and a tail (Linh), hippie beads and a loose tunic that actually doesn't look too different from what he usually wears (Alonso), or a T-shirt that's Clark Kent in the middle of changing into Superman (Enrique). Even the Creeper is dressed up as, I guess, some kind of a cowboy? He's wearing a cowboy hat, anyway. It takes me a minute to figure it out, but PJ is one of the characters from the super-gay cartoon we watched the night of the sleepover, and I hate that it took me a minute to figure it out and I also hate that I'm not dressed as another of the characters from the same show, and I especially hate that everyone immediately knows that PJ and I are fighting.

What happened was that I wanted to talk about PJ moving, but not *to* PJ, so I told Yesenia. Not just about the move itself but also about being there when her moms were fighting. Yesenia said they must be on a month-to-month to be able to move so fast, and I didn't know what she meant, but I pretended I did. And then I guess Yesenia told some other people, and it turned into PJ's moms definitely getting divorced, and also at the same time PJ being recruited for the Olympics, which I don't think is the way that works exactly?

Anyway, the point is that I thought PJ moving, itself, would be the hardest thing, but it turns out that when I got a text that said "Stop spreading my problems all over," and then I didn't get any answers to the twenty-seven texts I sent to apologize, that was worse.

And this is worse, too. I can't look at her but I can't *not* look at her, until she gets out lip balm, which I can't bear to watch her put on. Whatever flavor it is, I won't be tasting it.

Instead I look down at her shoes, a pair I drew on, not actually that long ago but it feels like it was. I didn't draw hearts or anything like that, just some stars and moons and music notes, because they're all easy to draw and also, I don't know, music and stars and moons can all be romantic but it's not like the only thing they can be, so it's a little more subtle? It doesn't matter now; the drawings have mostly worn away.

Alonso brings out the costume box in case there are littles who also need costumes, and there's a black cape that's maybe sort of vampirish, but mostly it's just giant and shapeless, like a tarp you'd put over something to protect it from rain, like some of the people who live in the ravine have for their tents. I take it—it's also the only thing that doesn't have buttons or zippers—and wish it would turn me invisible. Faisal points at the cape's Bend the Trend Resale price tag, still attached, and says, "Ha! Alex is five dollars! I wouldn't pay that!"

I yank off the tag and throw it at Faisal. The cape rips, because the cape is plastic. Now it looks like I've just draped myself in a literal garbage bag.

"We need to have a party for PJ, too!" says Yesenia. "Before she leaves us."

"Great idea!" says Alonso. "If that's what PJ wants, anyway," he adds, glancing over to where she's setting up the face-painting station. She looks like people in movies look when they're choosing which wire to cut to defuse a bomb. PJ is very good at face painting, but sometimes the littles won't stay still long enough for her to finish.

I wish I could ask her to paint my face.

I'd stay still.

I wouldn't even blink.

Then the littles swarm in, even though we're not ready, and Yesenia turns on her playlist and starts to dance, and a tiny person tugs on my cape and asks if I'm a monster.

I sweep the cape around myself and say yes.

I STAYED AFTER TO HELP CLEAN UP AND

also so that I could be very busy picking up scattered candy wrappers and silly string and somebody's jacket and somebody else's unicorn horn at the exact moment PJ was leaving the room.

Alonso stretches, reaching up to the ceiling, then twists at the waist. Then he yawns and says, "Whew! Thanks, Alex, that's a big help."

I want to tell him what's happening, but I don't know where

to start. I kind of want him to already know, and to know what I should do, and tell me, except not tell me exactly because it would be too hard to hear him talk about all the messed-up stuff.

Which makes me suddenly get why PJ's mad at me.

So instead of telling him anything at all, I just take off the ripped plastic tarp–cape and fold it and put it back in the costume box.

TEN

THERE WASN'T A PARTY. THEY JUST MOVED. I think Alonso has their new address, but I haven't asked him for it because I don't want him to know she didn't give it to me.

Yesenia told me after school Friday that I was obviously in need of some wholesome entertainment. "You're coming to my folklórico performance tomorrow, okay? We'll come get you. And also I need to come over sometime soon so you can show me the cat-sitting stuff."

She's going to feed Snufkin while Grandma and I are in Bend with Dad and Laura and the twins for Thanksgiving in a few weeks. She's very excited about cat-sitting, because she'll get to be in our house alone when she does it, and being alone is apparently a pretty rare phenomenon for her.

I've met Yesenia's mom before, and her brothers and little sister, but her dad is usually working. He's a contractor, so I'm kind of surprised to see that he's the one driving the minivan when they pull up in our driveway, but then I think I shouldn't be, because obviously he'd want to see her dance.

I squeeze in next to Yesenia and little Esperanza in the back row. As usual, I hate how much space my butt takes up, and also I wonder if any of them think it's weird that I brought my backpack, like we're going to school instead of to a dance concert. But I don't like purses—I don't even like the word—and I also don't like having things in my pockets, so I just default to the backpack, even though it probably makes it look like I'm either going to school or running away from home. I kind of hunch over, holding the backpack in front of myself like a shield.

"You all settled in back there? Got your seat belts fastened?" Yesenia's mom asks. I don't. I was too focused on just getting myself and my backpack situated, so now I have to awkwardly put the backpack down, reach for the belt, then dig around frantically for the buckle, which I finally find half-buried under Esperanza's car seat. Yesenia is also half-buried; she's holding a giant garment bag that instantly makes me think of my mom's dress, which makes me think of the *Merry Christmas from the Eagers* card, which is still in my backpack. So theoretically I could show it to Yesenia and ask her what she thinks is up with it.

But if I did, I'd have to explain to her more about my family, and I don't actually know all the things I might want to explain to her. And there's already a lot going on in the car: her brothers playing games on their phones, Esperanza singing loudly to herself, and the radio on in Spanish, I think a soccer game? I take Spanish, but the teacher talks a lot more slowly than the people on the radio. So I just say, "Settled! Thanks for inviting me!" and then stay quiet, breathing in Yesenia's mom's flowery perfume mixed with her brothers' body spray and the Virgen de Guadalupe air freshener hanging from the mirror, wondering what it's like to be in a family with this many people in it, and whether there's any stuff they don't talk about.

As we all come into the Grange, I can't help remembering the KKK photo PJ found, and it feels like when you bang into something hard with your knee and you know it's going to swell and bruise. But then I think about how mad those men would be about what's happening here today, and that makes me feel a little better.

A woman shrieks and crushes Yesenia and her garment bag into a huge hug. "Tía Gabi!" Yesenia says. "I love you and I have to get changed!" She charges away to wherever they've got set up as a dressing room, and it dawns on me that because I'm here to see Yesenia and she's going to be onstage, I'm not really here *with* anybody—anybody my own age, I mean—and I suddenly miss PJ so much I can't breathe.

Then Yesenia's mom says to come with her to pick up snacks for everyone, and I try to get out my wallet and she won't let me, but she does have me help carry the chips and drinks and napkins into the hall where everyone's starting to get seated, adults in folding chairs, little kids on the floor. There's Yesenia's tía, her dad, brothers and sister, and some other people in a cluster; I'm not sure if they're more relatives or not, but they all seem to have a lot to talk about.

I decide to save my chips, because they can be messy, but I'm thirsty, so I open my can of Coke—it fizzes and froths, of course, because it got shaken while I was carrying it, and I quickly slurp it up before it can get all over. My slurp sounds super loud to me, but no one else seems to notice. I set the can down carefully and text PJ, even though I know she won't answer:

> about to see yesenia's dance thing
>
> wish you were here

I take a picture of the banner hanging across the stage and send it to PJ, too.

> they have papel picado, remember that time in youth council when we made some?
>
> yours were so good, way better than mine

I watch the screen. *Sending* turns to *Sent* turns to *Delivered* turns to *Read*.

Then music starts, and it's time to look at the stage.

Yesenia and everyone onstage with her are wearing what look to me like fancy ruffly white curtains transformed into dresses. The dresses have such full skirts that the word *voluminous* comes into my head from last week's English vocabulary quiz. I wonder how to say voluminous en español; I want it to be voluminoso, but words aren't always cognates.

Thinking about words doesn't take my attention away from the stage, though. I guess a costume is always meant to sort of emphasize and enhance the thing you're wearing the costume for, but in this case, the dance literally could not be happening without the costumes, because a lot of what Yesenia and the others are doing with their arms is holding the skirts and swishing them around to make patterns. With all the fabric swirling, I can't believe no one has stepped on anyone else's skirt, or their own, for that matter.

I ended up sitting next to Yesenia's tía in one of the really uncomfortable plastic folding chairs, but fortunately I'm at the end of the row and have a wall on my other side so I can lean against it and not worry I'm crowding Tía Gabi—she said I should call her that. If anything, she's actually crowding me—her whole deal seems to be applauding and cheering, not just in between songs, but, like, continually throughout, like it's her job to make sure every person on the stage feels like they have at least one superfan. Every so often she nudges me to make sure I also do my share in the expressing-enthusiasm department.

My favorite dance turns out to be one that Yesenia's not in. It's just two adults, and again it's a dance that couldn't exist without the costumes. One of the dancers has a long, long sash. They stretch the sash out between them and drop it on the stage and start sort of gently kicking it, and I don't know why—I can only tell that they're moving the sash in very precise ways, using only their feet. Then they very gracefully bend down and pick it up and show it to the audience and I finally get it: They've tied the sash in a giant bow, which it absolutely did not occur to me was a thing you could do via dancing.

A lot of times when an adult is super enthusiastic like Tía Gabi, it makes me so embarrassed I feel like I've been scalded; like it's somehow dangerous even to be near someone who's showing that much feeling. But there's something about the way she's excited for everyone and everything that carries me along with her, and by the end of the show, I'm clapping and stomping as hard as she is.

My phone buzzes:

> big meet next sat

Then a link to a community center website with a schedule.

Maybe PJ didn't mean to send that, maybe it's one of those things where she meant to text it to someone else but because I texted her, she ended up replying to me by mistake?

I type:

> i'll be there.

ELEVEN

I DECIDED NOT TO ASK GRANDMA ABOUT whether I could go to Portland to see PJ's swim meet. I definitely wasn't going to ask her to drive me, because lately she doesn't like driving even just here in town, and to get to Portland she'd have to get on the highway. And I also definitely wasn't going to ask her if I could take the bus by myself, because obviously she'd say no.

So I looked up the route on my phone and figured out it'd take like an hour, but probably actually more like two hours because everything always takes longer than it seems like it should, and then I'll need another hour probably to get from the bus station to the community center where the meet is going to be, in case I get lost.

"Have you and Portia Jane had a falling out? You haven't mentioned her lately," Grandma says.

I choke on my mouthful of macaroni and cheese and have to take a big gulp of ice water before I answer.

"She's really busy with swimming," I say. It's not a lie.

WHEN I'M IN MY ROOM AND I SHOULD BE doing something else, like homework, I keep taking out the *Merry Christmas from the Eagers* card and staring at it. It wouldn't say *the Eagers* if the other kid was just a neighbor. But since Grandma hasn't ever said anything, does it mean he's dead, too? But a dead mom and a dead grandpa and a dead uncle just seem like a lot of dead relatives, so for some reason, instead of making me sad, it strikes me as ridiculous, like just sort of improbable? Then I think "A Lot of Dead Relatives" would make a good episode title for one of Grandma's mystery shows.

And I don't want to ask Grandma about the kid in the photo; I'm scared of what she might say.

Or not say.

What if she doesn't remember him?

WHEN YESENIA CAME OVER, I WAS PRETTY sure Grandma didn't remember that she'd met her before. Or that we'd already talked about her doing the cat-sitting. If Snufkin hadn't gotten all bizarrely loving toward her—like, more than he usually is with us—I don't think Grandma would've let me show her where we keep the extra house key, which is in one of those fake rocks that has a little compartment inside. It's by the front door, hidden among some real rocks.

"That's so cool! I want one," Yesenia says. "And you could use it for stuff besides keys. It'd have to be small stuff, but you could totally put like earrings?"

"Or your bracelet," I say.

Grandma's standing in the doorway near us, slightly frowning. "Have you taken care of animals before?"

Yesenia blushes, and so do I. I know why I'm blushing—it's because Grandma asked her that already—but I don't know why she is.

"Yes, our dog. And also my tía Gabi has two cats, and a lot of fish, actually? She has me feed them, too, any time she's out of town, and it's always gone really well." Yesenia says all this while she's still kneeling next to the fake rock, looking up at Grandma glaring down at her, and I don't like it. I was standing up, but I crouch down so I'll be on the same level as Yesenia, who's going on: "I don't know if you know, but fish are pretty complicated? You don't just dump in their food; you have to make sure the water is like it should be, too. I can handle Snufkin, no problem."

She didn't mention the fish before—is it that she thinks Grandma doesn't trust her? *Does* Grandma trust her?

"Well. You just please make sure to call if there's any trouble." Grandma shields her eyes to squint up at the sky. "Looks like we're in for some rain soon—you girls best get your outside time in before it hits. I'll get some supper on the table."

"Do you need help, Mrs. Eager?" asks Yesenia.

"Oh no. You go ahead and enjoy, before that rain hits." She shuts the door.

"Your grandma's nice," Yesenia says, and I'm so relieved that she said *nice* and not *weird* or anything worse that a bigger smile than I meant to smile takes over my face, and I look at the fake key-holding rock and the real rocks again so I don't have to look at her.

We decide to take a walk with the goal of petting as many dogs as possible. We get three right away, because the new neighbor, whose name Grandma told me is Mrs. Husselmann, is just taking hers out, two big poodles, Princess and Piper, and a little rat terrier, Tony. Princess and Piper are calm, Tony is jumpy and barky, but they all wag their tails and let us pet them after they sniff our hands. I'd probably have been scared if Yesenia hadn't explained that one time about how dogs do their jobs. Then I think about how I didn't want to go meet Mrs. Husselmann with Grandma. It's easier to talk to her now with Yesenia, because we're just talking about the dogs and how they're so good.

"If you were a dog, what kind of dog would you be?" Yesenia asks after we say goodbye to Tony, Princess, Piper, and Mrs. Husselmann. "A corgi," I say automatically. It's only after I say it that I remember PJ and I once had this same conversation, and it was her idea that I'd be a corgi: "Because they're sturdy and short and the absolute cutest!"

I wonder if she still thinks I'm the absolute cutest, or even cute at all.

"What about you?" I ask back, before my brain can totally take me away from right now with Yesenia into a fog of PJ memories and worry.

"I would be—hold on, let me find it—" Yesenia pulls out her phone. We walk a little more slowly while she scrolls; then she stops. "Ha! Yes! Here we go! I would personally like to be this exact chihuahua—look!" She shows me a really excellently dancing chihuahua, and then we have to watch more good animal videos. After that we keep walking and meet a sweet old yellow lab in a bandanna and a drooly sheepdog, and then, just like Grandma predicted, it starts to rain.

It makes me wonder how memory loss actually works, like, why would she lose people's names but not the sense for what's going to happen with the weather? Or maybe it's just that her weather sense hasn't gone yet, but it will? I don't want to think about it. Maybe it's not even all that big a deal. Grandma always says I overreact to stuff and that she wishes I weren't such a worrier.

A FEW DAYS BEFORE PJ'S MEET, BECAUSE

I'm trying to think of everything, I look up how old you have to be to travel on Greyhound by yourself.

Sixteen.

Otherwise known as three years older than I am.

You can be as young as twelve, but you have to have an Unaccompanied Child Form signed by an adult, with information about who's supposed to pick you up when you get to the place you're going, and the ticket has to be bought in person, so I can't just fake Grandma's signature on the form.

I think for a minute about asking Alonso to come and sign it for me, but I'm already sure he wouldn't do it; it'd get him in a lot of trouble at work probably, and he'd want to know why I'm not asking Grandma in the first place, and that is a conversation I do not want to have. And there aren't any other adults I'd even consider, except maybe Rachel or Kyla, but obviously that wouldn't work either because they're not in Failin anymore, so they couldn't come with me to buy the ticket.

But I need to be there. I promised PJ.

And the least I can do after spreading her problems all over is to keep my word.

Also I just miss her.

I still need to figure out where to tell Grandma I'm going to be. Maybe at Yesenia's? I don't want to get her in trouble, either. But then again, she's the one who told more people about PJ's moms fighting and PJ moving and everything.

As I'm thinking all this, I'm pacing. Like somehow my brain is convinced that if I walk back and forth enough times between my bed and the door, I'll suddenly know exactly how to make the trip go how I want.

But I can't think or pace my way into a perfect plan. I'm just going to get to the bus station on the day of her meet, early, with money for the ticket, and do whatever I have to do to get to Portland.

"I HAVE TO GO TO THE LIBRARY TO STUDY tomorrow," I tell Grandma at dinner the night before PJ's meet. "I'll probably be there all day, maybe even into the evening. I have a lot of work."

"You really think you'll need to be there all day? That doesn't sound good. Have you been getting behind on your assignments?"

"A little," I say. "The math we're doing now is confusing." I take a bite of pork chop that has a lot of the spice mix on it; sometimes it kind of clumps in places. The pepper burns my mouth as I chew.

"I know you don't think you should ever need to ask for help," says Grandma, "but sometimes it's better to ask than to struggle on your own." She reaches for the bowl of green beans to serve us both some more, and winces. "And if you're going to be on a study marathon, you remember to take breaks! Make sure you get up and stretch—you don't want to end up stiff all the time like me!"

My face gets hot. "Want me to do the Tiger Balm for your back after we eat?"

"Thank you, Alexandra, I'd appreciate it. That's very thoughtful."

We finish eating our green beans, pork chops, and rice. Grandma and I cooked together, which we sometimes do. I made the rice, and it came out good. It doesn't always, but this time I remembered to measure both the broth and the rice to make sure I had the ratio right, and to rinse the rice first. I snapped the ends off the green beans to get them ready to boil up, and I seasoned the pork chops the way she's taught me. You mix up the spices in a plastic bag, then put the pork chops in the bag and shake them so the spices get everywhere they need to be. Everything actually came out good, but I didn't enjoy it very much.

"I'll deal with the dishes first," I say, "and then I'll get the Tiger Balm."

"Well, then I'll just relax, I suppose!" Grandma bends down to pet Snufkin. He's weaving around her legs because he wants pork. We won't give him any, though; it's bad for cats.

"You should!" I say overly enthusiastically. Grandma makes a small *oof* sound as she stands up. Then she heads to her room, singing the line from "Mole in the Ground" about coming over the hill with a forty-dollar bill. I've never known if it means a forty-dollar bill like a twenty-dollar bill only worth twice as much, or a forty-dollar bill like you *owe* forty dollars.

We have a dishwasher, but it's old and not super powerful, so we always rinse everything before we load it. I make the water really hot and do a more thorough job rinsing than usual.

My hands are tingling when I finish. I get the Tiger Balm out of the medicine chest.

Grandma's lying on her bed on her stomach. I scoop out some Tiger Balm, then pull up her sweatshirt with my other hand and rub the red ointment carefully into her lower back. Camphor and menthol. The scent is so strong. When I breathe in, it feels like my lungs are getting scoured.

I focus on the familiar feeling of Grandma's back. She's strong, and big like me and like I guess my mom was, too, and her skin is soft even as I can tell the muscles underneath are tense and tight.

"Do you want some for your neck and shoulders, too?"

"That would be wonderful."

I scoop out some more. This time I start up at her collar, rubbing the balm in under her sweatshirt again, getting it on her neck and shoulders while avoiding her bra straps. I could move the straps out of the way, I guess, but it would feel weird and wrong.

I can really feel the tension in her neck and shoulders, the knots I used to think were actual knots like you might get in a shoelace. I press hard on one knot near her right shoulder.

"Ouch!"

"Sorry, I was just trying to get it to loosen up."

"Try again, now I'm braced for it."

I press down again on the knot and hold, and this time I think I can feel it release.

"Thank you, love," Grandma says. "Ah, it's kicking in. That helps."

"Good, I'm glad."

One of my eyes is watering. I rub it without thinking. It stings and stings and waters some more.

TWELVE

THE GREYHOUND STATION IS PRETTY CLOSE to FPL, so when I headed out, I was going the same direction I would have if I'd actually been going where I told Grandma I was going to be. She was still asleep when I left, and I felt bad about that, but also I didn't want to wake her up.

As I walked, I started having a new feeling. I can't put a name to it, but it's like when you go to a soda fountain and make a new drink out of different drinks. It tastes a little like being scared and a little like being excited and a little like how you feel when you do something you didn't think you could do. Even though I haven't really done anything yet, except get to the bus station. But I know at least part of where the feeling comes from: knowing that no one knows where I am right now.

The station is small and old, with too-bright fluorescent lights and bolted-down metal-and-plastic seats that remind me of the ones at Cedars Coin-Op Laundromat, where we went when the dryer was broken. They look like they're made on purpose to be too hard to sleep on.

I've been here before. We used to sometimes take the bus to

Bend to see Dad and Laura, which is why I should have probably remembered the thing about not being able to travel as an unaccompanied child, but those times I was always accompanied.

It was a cold walk, but that made me feel extra awake the whole way from our house. I got here so early that it's still pretty dark outside, and there are only a few other people waiting.

One of the waiting people looks like they're sleeping, even though the seats are hostile. They look like they're maybe in their twenties? Eyes closed, long lashes, silver glitter eye shadow, olivey skin, thick well-shaped dark brown eyebrows, traces of dark lipstick. I can't see their hair, because they're wearing a black hoodie and a big set of headphones over the hoodie. I wonder if the headphones are the kind that block out sound. They also have a big army-green duffel bag, and their legs are propped up on it, which I guess must make the whole setup a little more comfortable. The duffel is heavily written and drawn on in black marker. Some phrases I think are probably band names, like Booty Gold and the Tasteful Pirates. One sentence really catches my attention: *ASK ME ABOUT MY GAY AGENDA.* The word *gay* is outlined in blue glitter—maybe nail polish? Or it could be glitter glue. Whatever kind of glitter it is, there's a lot of it, and it makes me smile.

As I'm smiling, the person with the duffel bag yawns and stretches and opens their eyes. "Hey." Their voice is medium deep and sounds a little like they have a cold. "What time is it?"

I tell them. They crack their neck and yawn again. "Mind watching my bag a minute?"

"Sure," I say, trying to sound casual. Then I blurt out, "Actually, can I ask you a favor also? I mean, when you get back?" My voice is higher pitched and my words are coming out faster than I want them to.

"Hold that thought," they say, and grin. They get up and stretch again. They're a small person, but they have a big presence. The smoldery way they grin, especially, makes me feel like they're letting me in on a secret, and for a wild moment I think I'm getting a crush on them? I'm blushing, because of course I'm blushing. "I'll just be a few minutes," they tell me, and saunter away.

While they're gone, I keep looking at their bag. I don't understand a lot of the references, and there are some symbols, too, that I don't recognize. But I do see a quote from a book I like, and it's near *ASK ME ABOUT MY GAY AGENDA*.

"All right, so tell me about this favor. I'm Harper, by the way," Harper says. They sprawl back into the seat directly across from me, cocking one leg over the chair arm and folding the other underneath them, like they're doing a yoga pose specifically designed for bus stations.

I take a deep breath. "I'm Alex. And I need to get to Portland to see my girlfriend, but I'm thirteen, and there's a thing where you can't take the bus until you're sixteen unless you're traveling with an adult."

"And you want me to be your adult?"

I nod, hating that my blush has fully returned, and decide that since I'm already blushing anyway, I might as well get extra brave. "I thought it might fit with your agenda," I say, pointing to Harper's duffel.

Harper's smoldery grin comes back. "It absolutely does."

It turns out that Harper has already bought their own ticket, which makes me worry that it'll look suspicious when they come up with me to the counter, but they're very smooth. "Alex here is traveling with me," Harper says. The guy at the counter asks, "And you're how old?" "Eighteen," Harper says, and "Thirteen," I say at the same time. "All right, it's full fare for you, young lady," the guy says to me. I hand him the cash, he hands me the ticket, and we're done.

"Thank you so much, this is really—I'm just really grateful," I say as we're standing in line to board.

"What would you have done if I hadn't been here?" Harper asks. We're the same height, so they're looking directly into my eyes as they ask, and the eye contact is too much, so I look at their duffel again and try to memorize phrases and symbols so I can look them up later.

"I don't know," I say, which is, simply, true. "Um, why are you, I mean, why were you here, if you don't mind my asking? Failin doesn't have a lot going on, really." Even as I say those words, they don't seem right—Failin does have a lot going on, like the city council election and how it might affect how the budget gets spent, and the people who live in the ravine trying to stay warm and dry as winter starts to come in. I guess what I really mean is that the things Failin has going on aren't the kinds of things people tend to travel for.

"It was on the way," Harper says. I wait to hear where Failin is on the way to—I mean, I'm guessing it's Portland, but maybe Portland is just a stop along the way also—but Harper doesn't tell me. We shuffle forward a little in line. Harper kicks the duffel bag forward, too, and says, "I firmly believe you have to stop sometimes in places you wouldn't necessarily seek out. They can surprise you."

ONCE WE'RE SEATED, HARPER PUTS THEIR

headphones back on and falls asleep almost instantly. For a minute I think they're faking because they don't want to talk to me, but I don't think anybody could fake those loud, irregular snores. They remind me of Grandma's snores, and that makes me wonder if she's woken up yet, and if she remembers I told her I'd be at the library.

I shove those thoughts away.

But Harper being asleep means I'm alone with my brain, and I can't stop spinning stories: PJ wins all her events, I race out of the stands, and we kiss right by the pool while she's still in her bathing suit, and then I offer her my coat so she doesn't get chilled. Or: PJ sees me in the stands, glares, shakes her head and won't even talk to me. Or: I can't ever even find the community center, and I just wander around Portland helplessly until it's time to go back to the bus station, and maybe I miss the bus, also.

Which is when it hits me: I was so afraid I wouldn't be allowed to buy a ticket at all—and, let's be honest, I was so flustered by Harper, my knight in shining glitter—that I bought a one-way.

I GUESS IT SHOULDN'T SURPRISE ME THAT

the community center is bigger and fancier than the Failin Grange Hall. For one thing the walls are freshly painted. One is purple, one bright yellow, and a third has a mural, the kind I know is supposed to make you feel like it's really super communityish because lots of different kids painted different parts of it. But I always hate those kind of murals, because some parts are just way better done than others.

And if I stare hard at the tail of this one red fish in the corner and get irritated that whoever painted it just didn't even bother finishing the scales, it means I'm not thinking about how scared I am that coming here was a mistake.

It suddenly seems really important that PJ not see me until afterward. Maybe I should have worn a disguise. And Kyla and Rachel are probably here, too, somewhere; I can't let them see me, either.

I follow other people; we make our way past a room with exercise machines and another room with weights to the pool.

The pool is big. I resent its bigness, because its Olympic size is part of why PJ had to move. But I push that feeling aside. I buy a heat sheet, a water, and a breakfast burrito and find a space in the back row of the bleachers, just as I see Kyla and Rachel coming in to find seats, too. *Don't look up,* I tell them silently, but then again why would they? We're all here to look at the water, and specifically at PJ in it.

PJ's in four events: two relays and two individuals, the 100-meter butterfly and the one she told me she loves the most, the 100-meter individual medley. Individual medley is where you swim all the different kinds of strokes—butterfly, backstroke, breaststroke, and freestyle—and it's basically only the best swimmers who swim it. (PJ didn't tell me that; Kyla and Rachel did.)

Just carefully highlighting her name on the heat sheet makes my heart speed up like it's competing in its own event.

And when I catch sight of her on the pool deck, wearing a new black swimsuit and the same neon-blue swim cap that I can never believe her hair fits under, her arms looking somehow even stronger, muscles more defined than they were the last time I saw her, my heart sets what she's told me is called a PR, a personal record: It's never beat so fast.

Watching her in the butterfly, knowing she doesn't know I'm here yet, I want to cheer as hard for her as Tía Gabi did for Yesenia and everyone, but I also don't want to distract her. I mean, I don't even know if she'd be able to hear me, what with being in the water and making her own noise and the crowd yelling in the bleachers, but a probably self-centered part of me thinks she could? And I also kind of don't want to cheer in case it turns out she can't tell it's me cheering for her, or, worse, if she can and she doesn't want me to be here. So instead I sit very still and cross my fingers and watch PJ pull and kick through the water, up and down, so smooth and strong, and I don't cheer.

I don't breathe, either, not until she wins, and then I can't stop myself from jumping up and clapping until my hands sting, and I lose what's left of my breakfast burrito because I forgot it was in my lap and it fell all the way under the bleachers, but I don't care.

I think she might see me? She looks into the bleachers and waves a little, but maybe she was waving at Rachel and Kyla. Then one of PJ's teammates, who's very cute, hugs her, and at first, I think well okay, they're teammates, it's like a team-bonding hug. But then it seems like it goes on longer than a team-bonding hug would, not that I'd actually know anything about that since I've never been on a team, unless you count Youth Council, and we do not do team-bonding hugs. Anyway it's just a really long hug, and I feel like throwing up.

Then for a long stretch people who aren't PJ are doing events, and all I can do is dwell on that hug. I try to tune into details to distract myself: the chloriney scent of the air, the view of the crowded parking lot through the wall of windows opposite the bleachers, two people having an argument outside a big red minivan, a squirrel darting across the bright blue paint marking a disabled parking space, the drizzly rain that's started falling, the people near me, who are the parents of someone named Aidan, and Aidan isn't having his best day, they know they should've gotten him to go to sleep earlier, but he was so keyed up. *Keyed up* makes me think of a clockwork toy being overwound, or the side of a car that someone has angrily scratched.

And then it's the medley relay and her team loses, and I'm angry at whichever slow swimmer was dragging them down. Maybe it was the cute one; it clearly wasn't PJ. And then it's stressfully boring for a long time. I need to pee, but if I get up, I might miss her individual medley, where she'll swim all the different strokes. My brain fixates on the word *stroke* and the concept of stroking, and I have to put my hands over my cheeks because they're so hot and red.

Finally it's time for PJ's individual medley. I don't know if she's already faster and better than she was in Failin with our wrong-sized pool, but it seems like she probably is, and I'm glad I get to see her do this thing she does so well.

She wins.

And now I can get up and find the bathroom.

I'm washing my hands and wondering if I've missed her team's other relay when a hand is suddenly on my shoulder.

"Alex? Kiddo? Where did you come from?"

It's Kyla.

Part of me wants to say *Failin*, but that would be what Grandma calls *smart-alecky*, which I used to think was because my name's Alex, but then I saw it in a book, so I guess it isn't. I say "Hi!" and then get very busy rubbing my hands under the hand dryer, which is very loud.

"PJ didn't say you were going to be here. You should come sit with us!"

She seems happy to see me, which is nice; I was kind of afraid PJ had told them I'd been gossiping about them and they'd never want to see her again.

But she didn't tell them I was coming—does that mean she definitely doesn't want me here? Because I did text her I was coming, but she never answered. Oh no.

"It's a surprise," I say quickly. "So I'll find you after, but I shouldn't sit with you in case she's, um, looking for you in the stands and sees me, okay? I better get back, bye!"

I didn't even eat all of the breakfast burrito I bought, since it fell off my lap earlier when I stood up to clap for PJ, but I spend the rest of the meet regretting having had any of it, while I try to suppress the belches that anxiety keeps propelling up from my stomach to my throat. I'm sure my breath is awful. Why didn't I bring breath mints?

PJ's team wins their second relay, the freestyle one, and that's great, I guess. But when I see them all hugging again, and giving each other high fives on the pool deck, I'm sure that she's already happier with her team than she ever was with me. Probably especially with the cute one.

When the meet is finally over, I almost don't want to go and find Kyla and Rachel. But then I remember how I only got a one-way bus ticket, and I don't actually know when I need to get to the station to buy a return, if I even can without the magic of Harper and their glittery agenda.

Before I get up, I rummage in my backpack, and at the very bottom I turn up an old stick of gum. Fortunately, it's still wrapped, and even more fortunately, it's peppermint. But chewing is sort of gross and cowlike, so I'll just chew for a little while for the flavor, and then I'll get rid of the gum.

"What a nice surprise!" Rachel says when I come up to her and Kyla. She pats me on the shoulder in a way I'd find annoying if it were anyone else. "She'll be getting out of the locker room any minute now. Let's go meet her."

It's crowded outside the locker room, mostly with parents and siblings, I think. Some people are holding up phones, I guess to capture the exact moment their person emerges, and some have water and energy drinks and snacks.

I get rigid.

It's hard to breathe.

Or move.

I do manage to swallow my gum.

And then there she is, wearing the gray fleecy hoodie I got her for her birthday last year, and seeing it makes me feel like maybe it's going to be okay because if she still likes the hoodie maybe she still likes me, and she shrieks, and then we're hugging hugging hugging, and I can smell the peppermint shampoo she uses to get chlorine out of her hair and feel stupidly glad that my gum was the same flavor, and my cheek is smushed into her shoulder and the soft fleece feels like a security blanket and her arms are so strong and I still can't quite believe she's not still mad at me but here we are.

My phone starts ringing. The only person who calls me instead of texting is Grandma. I know I should pick up, but I can't let go of PJ yet, not when I thought I might never get to hold on to her like this again, so I let it ring.

"Big surprise, huh?" Rachel ruffles PJ's hair, and we step away from each other as though Rachel's hair-ruffling was a Stop Hugging signal.

"Let's get out of here, champ! You hungry?" says Kyla. We start walking out to the parking lot.

"Yes! I need to eat all the foods! Can we go to Fuel, please?" PJ reaches for my hand and I take it. We're holding hands! Not only is she glad I'm here, she still wants to hold hands! In public!

"They have the best scrambles and potatoes, Alex," she says. "They're so good it's ridiculous."

That gives me a weird pang. How can she already have a new favorite restaurant? Has she forgotten how good the food is at Vince's 24 Hours?

Then my phone starts ringing again.

I fumble to silence it just as a text comes in from Alonso. Did I forget a Youth Council thing?

> Alex, call me as soon as you see this.

For a dumb moment I think, *He wants to say hi to PJ!* and then I remember that he doesn't know I'm with PJ, that in fact no one knows I'm with PJ except PJ and Rachel and Kyla.

"Where's your grandma, Alex?" Kyla's voice is quiet, but it has that tone—you hear it from teachers sometimes—that means that if you lie to them, they'll know.

So the best thing to do is not lie: "She didn't come with me."

We've gotten out to their car now, the dark blue Subaru with the rack on top for their bikes, and I think about how many times I've ridden in it.

Rachel frowns. "And no one else came with you, either, did they? How did you even— God, you're not going to tell me you hitchhiked, are you? That's not even— Never mind. Alex. Your grandma doesn't know you're here, does she?"

"I didn't hitchhike," I say. Then, because getting home suddenly seems more important than it did a minute ago: "Can you take me to the bus station?"

"We have to eat first," says PJ. "Please, Alex came all the way here, and we haven't even barely gotten to talk to each other!"

Rachel pushes a button on her key ring, and the car doors thunk unlocked. PJ gets into the back seat without letting go of my hand, so I get in, too, even though I don't know if Kyla and Rachel actually want me to.

"Did the two of you plan this—this escapade together?" Rachel asks.

I thought I'd thought about everything, but I did not think for one single moment about how Rachel and Kyla would react when I showed up.

"No," I say. "It was all me. I, um, excuse me, though, for a minute—I have to make a call?"

My voice squeaks on *call*. It's actually the last thing I want to do, but since I told Grandma I was going to be at FPL, and Alonso works for FPL, I guess she must have come to the library to look for me? And talking to Alonso feels a little bit easier than talking to Grandma or Kyla or Rachel right now, so I scroll through my short list of contacts and tap my thumb on his name.

Kyla's behind the wheel but hasn't started the engine. Rachel is in the passenger seat twisting her head back to look at us, like we might somehow be able to get up to something nefarious if she breaks eye contact. Alonso picks up right away. "Alex! Are you okay? Where are you? We need to—we need to have a conversation about your grandma before you talk to her."

"Is she okay?" Now my voice is wobbly. *Thoughtless, thoughtless, thoughtless* repeats in my head, a word Grandma doesn't use often but I'm still hearing it in her voice, and I want to say back to the Grandma voice in my head that it's not that I'm thoughtless, it's just that all my thoughts were of PJ, who's squeezing my hand right now.

"Well . . ." Alonso says, and he sighs—I can hear it. "Well, let me back up. Are you okay?"

"Yes. I'm with PJ and her moms in Portland. But they didn't know I was coming!" I say this part for Rachel and Kyla's benefit, in case they're thinking I'm going to try to make it look like it's their fault that I'm not with Grandma when she needs me. I squeeze PJ's hand back and go on: "I did it for a surprise and I took the bus and I was going to come back just later today? But what's happened to Grandma?"

"Put him on speaker, Alex," Rachel says in her own version of the unrefusable teacher voice.

I do and hold the phone up like I want everyone to hear a song I love, except I'm sure it's going to be basically the opposite.

Alonso sighs again, which is strange to hear on speaker. "She came here, to the library," he says slowly.

"Looking for me?" I ask, already sure that's why, but for some reason feeling like I should say it out loud.

"Well, that might've been why she set out," Alonso says. He pauses. For a while. I can hear him breathing.

I'm cold all over, and my hand in PJ's goes slack.

"But, ah," he goes on finally, "it seems she got confused somewhere along the way. She showed up at the staff entrance for Tech Services, and when Ann let her in, she, well, she got pretty upset that her cubicle wasn't there."

"Oh," I say. Now Kyla has turned around, too. We've just been sitting in the parking lot this whole time, and the rain's started up again harder, battering down loud on the Subaru's roof like the roof is a big door and dozens of tiny people are knocking on it hard, trying to get in.

It's been three years since Grandma retired.

Alonso knows that, of course.

"What should I do?" I ask.

I don't know who I'm asking.

THIRTEEN

RACHEL AND KYLA MADE A PLAN WITH Alonso that they'd drive me back, but not until after we got food, because PJ was about to pass out, she said, even though she had a protein bar while we were talking to Alonso.

No one answered the question about what I should do. Alonso told me there was a lot more to talk about, but it would need to wait until the conversation could happen in person. Which, normally I would have been angry about him being so vague and mysterious, but when he said it, I just felt like I had gotten a tiny reprieve from whatever else still needs to be discussed, which obviously isn't going to be anything good. I do try calling Grandma, because Rachel tells me I need to, but she doesn't pick up, and that is both concerning and a relief.

So now we're at that Fuel place where PJ wanted to go, and I wish I felt like eating anything, but I really don't. It does seem like a good restaurant. I can smell strong coffee and bacon and potatoes; it's cozy and has nice sturdy chairs, and the waitstaff are friendly.

I didn't want to assume Rachel and Kyla would pay so I just

got a Coke, and its sweet carbonated burn is sort of comforting. But also I wish I'd gotten hot chocolate or really anything hot, because it's gotten chillier with the rain, and I just have my jean jacket over a T-shirt.

I shiver.

Probably because I haven't said anything since we got off the phone with Alonso, PJ and Rachel and Kyla have started talking about the meet and the girls on PJ's team, the ones who've been nice and the ones who've been mean. Rachel is sure the mean ones are jealous because PJ's so good at swimming. "Maybe?" PJ says. "But honestly I think they'd be mean regardless. If I wasn't fast, they'd be mean because I was slow."

The fact that they're talking about the meet is giving me a reprieve inside Alonso's reprieve from having to talk about Grandma. I thought they'd want to ask me a million questions about how long she's been forgetful and whether her forgetting things has gotten in the way of "the activities of daily living," which is a phrase I know because, even though I haven't talked to anyone about Grandma, I've been trying to read about memory loss online.

But I can't do it for very long before I get sad. And rigid.

Then all three of them go silent and look at me, as though by being grateful for the reprieve I've jinxed actually having one.

"I'm really glad you came, still," says PJ. "And I'm sorry about your grandma. Maybe it was just a weird day for her for some reason?"

"Yeah, maybe," I say, but I know that's not it. What I can't figure out is why Grandma didn't want to talk to me, I mean after the calls where I didn't pick up. Alonso said we'd talk in person.

Did my coming here make her get way worse?

"Kiddo, you should get some protein in you. Here, take the other half of my sandwich," says Kyla.

It's a BLT, which can be really good or pretty awful, depending on how it's made. I still don't feel hungry, but I take a bite to be polite and it turns out it's a really good BLT, perfectly toasted bread, bacon crisp the way I like it, lettuce not wilted, a tomato that tastes like a tomato and not like wet mush. I find an appetite after all.

Then Kyla wants to know what's happening with city council and the budget, and I confess that I'm not really sure.

"I'm not optimistic," says Rachel. "With that creep from Heritage coming on, and— Oh, babe, who's the other new one? The real estate agent, the one you went to high school with? Her hair always looks shellacked?"

"Tammy Ferguson."

Kyla grew up in Failin but moved away for school, I remember PJ telling me at some point. School was where she met Rachel, and Kyla's parents weren't too happy about the whole situation of them getting together. They were freaked out about having a lesbian daughter, and then extra freaked out because Rachel's Jewish and Kyla grew up going to the Heritage Bible Church, and after she and Rachel started dating, she stopped. Apparently things improved with them after PJ was born, but I remember Rachel saying that Kyla's family barely wants to admit she exists. I bet Rachel's really happy they moved away. I wonder if Kyla is.

PJ asks, "Have you been talking more in Youth Council? Do you know what you'll do if city council messes with the library budget?"

I don't want to tell her that I actually skipped the last Youth Council meeting because I was too sad about her being gone and not speaking to me, and I didn't want anyone to ask me how she was doing and have to make something up.

I feel furious at myself that I don't know anything about city council, or about what we should do if they do something bad, and that feeling stacks on top of the *thoughtless, thoughtless, thoughtless* feeling about abandoning Grandma to come here, and also the giant embarrassed feeling about messing up PJ's moms' whole day by making it so they have to drive me back, like they're all ingredients in a terrible sandwich of awful feelings that I've shoved down my throat along with the BLT. I take a sip of my Coke, but its burn doesn't help. I didn't really think it would.

Then the waiter, whose dark eyeliner makes me think of Harper, comes up with the bill. "No rush, take as long as you like."

"Thanks, but we need to head out," says Kyla, handing over a credit card.

"I HAVE TO SHOW YOU SOMETHING," I SAY

to PJ. We're about halfway to Failin, and so far we've talked about PJ's new school, which is scarily giant, and how not-unpacked they are, and how the house they're in has a bunch of stuff in it that belongs to one of her moms' friends who's on sabbatical and traveling for a whole year, and how much she likes her new coach, and how much we've been missing each other.

I can't regret coming. Even though I'm worried about Grandma. Even though I feel bad for Rachel and Kyla having to drive me home, especially because while me and PJ have been holding hands and catching up, they've been having a low-level fight about whether they need to stop and see Kyla's parents before they go back to Portland.

I can't regret it, not when PJ and me are back to being ourselves again, how we can talk about anything.

I tell her about finding my mom's dress and the jewelry box in the cedar chest. "So this was in the box," I say, taking the *Merry Christmas from the Eagers* card out of my backpack. It's still in the ziplock bag I put it in, plus I stuck it between the pages of a book so it wouldn't get banged up. "And I don't know who this is." I show her the card and point to the kid who isn't my mom.

"Whoa. Your grandma's never said anything about having another kid?"

I shake my head.

"Huh. That's a lot." She keeps examining the photo, holding it closer. "Well, he'd be grown up now, so you have to imagine, like, an adult version of the face? And it's weird, but I don't know, he does look like I should know him? But maybe that's just because he looks like you? They both do."

I hadn't thought about that. I mean, I guess I look enough like my mom for Grandma to confuse me with her, but I hadn't thought about how the other kid has similar features, too—the nose, the cheeks. And they're both smiling, but the smiles look kind of frozen and fake, like mine in school pictures.

As Kyla pulls into the parking lot, I have a moment of thinking, *Wait, why are we going to the library and not my house?* Then it comes back to me: Right, it's because Alonso has to tell me something in person before I see Grandma, who is for some reason still at the library and not home.

"So much for grading any papers today," Rachel says as the four of us get out of the car.

"They're all in the cloud, though, right, Mom? You could grade them on your phone," says PJ.

"Maybe *you* could," says Rachel. "That is not something my eyes and thumbs could handle."

FPL is usually a comforting place, but now I don't want to climb the concrete steps to the main entrance of the old brick building or use the ramp that the skateboarders like. I want to go somewhere totally different, with PJ.

There used to be bushes right under the big front windows, but people would hide in them, or hide stuff in them—or maybe both, I don't remember—but whichever, FPL had to cut them down. Youth Council was going to plant something else where the bushes were, but we couldn't agree on whether we should do flowers or vegetables, and I think after a while Alonso forgot we'd wanted to do it at all.

It's almost dark already. I don't want to go in, but I also don't want Grandma to have to drive home in the dark.

I start up the ramp, PJ following me.

"They have computers you can use here," I say to Rachel, trying to be helpful. "And thank you again for driving me back," I say to Kyla. "I really appreciate it."

"They do have computers, don't they? Hey, you know what?" Rachel's talking to Kyla now. "Why don't I stay here and work while you and PJ visit—that way I won't be so behind."

"I want to stay with Alex," says PJ. She takes my hand again. Hers is much warmer than mine.

"Not in the cards, kid," Kyla says. "Alex has things to do. We've got your grandparents to visit. They'll want to hear all about the meet and how well you did."

Suddenly I'm extremely tired. I guess I did get up really early to get to the bus station.

I wonder where Harper is by now.

PJ looks like she's about to start arguing with Kyla, so before she can get into it, I give her a giant hug.

"I should go in," I say. "I'll text you about how everything goes."

And then I go in.

FOURTEEN

ALONSO WAS WAITING FOR ME RIGHT INSIDE. "Hey there," he said. "We can talk in the Youth Council room. How does that sound?"

I nodded.

"Okay," says Alonso once we're in the storage closet. He has to keep the door open, because, as he's explained, it's policy to do that when he's alone with a minor. But it's at least more private than if we were standing out in the middle of the library, where anybody walking by could hear what we were saying.

"This is going to be a lot to take in," he continues. He's leaning against the wall. I'm standing with my arms crossed over my chest, staring at my shoes.

"I know what dementia is," I say. "I've been reading about it online."

I haven't read enough, though. I haven't looked up what all her prescriptions are for like I meant to, because I had to figure out how to get to Portland.

I'm the worst and most selfish person who has ever existed.

"That's, uh, that's part of it, yes, and I'm glad you've been getting some information. There are some good books about being a caregiver, too. You know I can always help you find more, uh, resources," he says.

"Because it's literally your job," I say, which is a joke we make all the time in Youth Council. We ask him about some totally random thing like whether llamas can smell flowers, and if he doesn't want to get us off topic by taking the time to find an answer, someone will always say, "Um, excuse me but you *have* to, because it is *literally* your job."

"Yes." Alonso half smiles. Then he walks over to the bulletin board, takes down a flier Linh made for the Halloween party, puts it in the recycling.

"But there's another thing we're dealing with here," he goes on, "besides your grandma's memory. Uh, you know how sometimes when you have a big disagreement with someone you really care about, it can last a long time?"

"It wasn't that long! PJ and I are great again now," I say, remembering how hard she hugged me, how much time she spent holding my hand.

But as soon as I say it, I know that's not what Alonso's talking about. He scratches the back of his neck where sometimes the hair tries to escape from his ponytail.

I dig into my backpack and find, again, the *Merry Christmas from the Eagers* card. I hand it to Alonso. "You're talking about this person. Right? The one who's not my mom?"

"I've never seen—wow! Those sweaters! Sorry, Alex," he says, "I just wasn't expecting you to— So she must have talked about him to you after all?"

"No. I just found the card," I say.

Another library person is suddenly in the doorway, a middle-aged lady who always has dresses with cool patterns, like squids or crossed swords or unicorns. Today it's corgis. I think she's Alonso's boss. She hasn't been here super long; she started after Grandma retired. "Hey, I hate to interrupt," she says, "but Chris is going home sick, so I'm gonna need you to cover the desk."

Alonso pulls on his ponytail like he's trying to yank his hair completely out of his scalp. "Let me just walk Alex over to the meeting room first, okay?"

The meeting room, the bigger one where we had the party for the littles, usually has something going on in it, but I guess it doesn't right now. Or actually, I guess Grandma is what's going on.

"Oh that's a good idea. Hi, Alex," she says. I am 100 percent sure she wouldn't have known my name if Alonso hadn't just used it. Of course, I don't know hers, so I don't know why I feel like she should have known mine, except that I come to FPL all the time and am on Youth Council and Grandma used to work here. I guess I feel like maybe everyone who works at the library at least kind of knows me? Which makes it all that much worse that Grandma is having trouble here, and it's obviously my fault.

Corgi-Dress Lady goes back to wherever she came from, and Alonso hands me back the *Merry Christmas from the Eagers* card. "Okay," he says. "I'd hoped to have longer to build up to this, but, uh, yeah. You have an uncle. He's the boy in that photo, and he's with your grandma now. They're waiting for you in the meeting room."

"JUST WHO DO YOU THINK YOU ARE, YOUNG lady?" That's the first thing Grandma says when I come into the meeting room.

I want to know who she thinks I am, too, but it's not a question I can ask.

She's sitting at the same table where PJ was doing the face painting.

The other person with her is the Creeper.

"Alex," he says, "you really worried your grandma."

You mean your mom, I want to say, and it makes me think of all the "your mom" jokes that kids constantly make, because insulting a mom is, I guess, even funnier than insulting the person themselves. One time Mark Hetzel said, "Your mom's so fat—" and I said, to cut him off, "She's dead," and then he said, "Your mom's so fat she's dead!" And he laughed and laughed.

"Who even are you?" I ask the Creeper. "Don't you work here? Shouldn't you be working?"

"Alex!" Grandma says. "That's not how you speak to—"

"I'm Dean," says the Creeper. Then he puts his hand out for me to shake, which is so awkward, and yet my hand goes out to meet his, and I notice his ring—it's a sort of dark gray shiny stone that I think is pretty and is also somehow familiar? I don't know why.

Hematite, that's what it's called. It's supposed to be healing, I know from when Yesenia got super into reading about the properties of different kinds of stones and crystals.

His hand is warm; the handshake is firm. This is my mom's

brother, and I don't know why I don't already know him. What did he do to make Grandma erase him from her life, and mine?

"I have a lot more to say to you," says Grandma.

Both of us turn to her.

"But not out in the middle of everything, public like a frog."

"Public like a frog" is from one of her favorite poems, by Emily Dickinson. Why can she remember it? None of this makes any kind of sense.

Dean—Uncle Dean, it sounds so strange in my head—says, "I can drive you home," and Grandma says, "No need. You're working," and he says, "I'll take the rest of the day off. We're only open another hour."

Grandma gets up, which amazes me. Dean takes out his phone and texts someone—I bet the corgi-dress lady, since she's probably his boss, too. Which makes me want to text PJ, but if I do, it'll just make Grandma angrier, and besides, I know we're not done with whatever all this is going to be.

On our way out, Alonso gives us a little wave from the reference desk, and I wish he hadn't. It's not that I mind him knowing things about my family, exactly; it's just that until now he's been in a different category, separate from home. How can I keep being on Youth Council when Alonso knows I should be home helping Grandma all the time?

"I'll need the keys," the Creeper Uncle Dean says to Grandma at the car.

It comes to me all of a sudden: Those times I saw him watching me, he wasn't watching because he's a creeper. He was watching because he's my uncle, and he wanted to know me.

I still want to know what he did, though.

It had to have been really bad for Grandma to be mad at him for my whole life.

Until now, I guess.

Or was it him being mad at her?

"Is your license up to date?" Grandma asks. "What about accidents?"

"Not so much as a parking ticket," says Uncle Dean. He sounds overly calm, like making-a-big-effort, on-purpose calm, like when he was talking to the wine-box drunk guy.

"Well, I hope you don't still ride the gas," Grandma says, and hands him the keys.

Seeing her in the passenger seat, seeing Uncle Dean behind the wheel, makes me feel like I need a seat belt besides the one I'm already wearing.

I thought there'd be yelling, but both Uncle Dean and Grandma are totally quiet, except for once when he brakes a little abruptly at a light and Grandma sucks her teeth in, a little hiss.

Maybe Grandma won't start yelling until after Uncle Dean leaves our house.

For the dumbest split second I think, *I don't even know his last name*, but of course I do.

I wonder if he got teased about the name Eager, too.

I wonder if my mom did.

I wonder what he can tell me about her.

I wonder what will happen next.

> turns out the Creeper is actually my uncle

WHAT

> ikr
>
> his name is Dean

but what

I mean

w

t

actual

f

> i don't know
>
> they didn't really tell me anything???
>
> except that I'm grounded
>
> which is not a surprise
>
> and i guess uncle dean wants to like get to know me or whatever

UNCLE DEAN!!??!

> well it's his name
>
> and he's my uncle

how did your grandma never say

how did HE not say

anything

ever

your grandma even worked for the library right??

so they literally even WORKED in the same PLACE so how did they not

> i don't know when he started, it might have been after she retired? besides, grandma was in tech services and they're in the basement, so they didn't really see people who worked in, like, the main part

oh. i guess that makes sense

how are you like doing though

like

with

like

everything

> well I miss you again already

SAME

> and it's weird

> and i'm still really worried

> but i also don't know what i can actually do, yet?

> there's a lot to figure out

> yeah that sounds hard

> i'm sorry

PJ sends a string of hug emojis. Then:

> are you going to tell people?

> like yesenia?

It's just words on a screen, obviously, but I can hear in that text how even though PJ isn't still mad at *me*, she's definitely still mad. I want to apologize again, but also I don't want to get into a whole thing? So I just type:

> i don't know

Which is true. And then:

> oh one other thing about uncle dean, i have his phone number now? i don't know when i would use it exactly but he wanted me to have it

> he has mine now too

> that's weird

> i mean

> not weird I guess

> because you ARE related

> but i can't get used to this library rando being part of your family

> i mean he was always part of it i just didn't know until now

> also
>
> if you can't get used to it how do you think i feel

Then it's just the three dots for a long time. Finally PJ sends some hearts and I send some hearts back, and I guess that means we're done texting for a while.

I can hear Grandma moving around in the kitchen, probably cleaning up the dinner dishes. Uncle Dean said he could do them, but Grandma said, "I don't want to hold you up," which is a thing she says when she actually wants someone to go away, and I think Uncle Dean must have known, because not long after she said that, he left.

Before, when Grandma said she wasn't going to let him go away hungry and got out leftover mac and cheese to warm up, he was the one who set the table. He knew where everything was in the cabinets.

He stood in front of the one with all her prescriptions in it for a long while before he reached for the drinking glasses.

While we ate, Grandma told me I can't lie to her like that again, that doing what I did wasn't just deceptive, it was dangerous. Uncle Dean stayed quiet.

I wanted to ask, *If I hadn't done it, would I have ever found out I have an uncle?*

I didn't, of course. I just said I was so sorry. And I was, and I am.

But sorry isn't the only thing I'm feeling.

I started noticing ways the three of us looked alike: full cheeks, the arch of our eyebrows, even the way our hair grows, although it's harder to tell since Grandma's is white and Uncle Dean's is kind of salt-and-pepper. But it's the same hair, somehow, especially since the pepper in Uncle Dean's is actually a lot like the medium brown of mine. And we also move alike, like the way Uncle Dean reaches for the water pitcher looks like the way Grandma reaches for it which also looks like the way I reach for it, and we all do the thing of dabbing at our lips with our napkins like we're blotting lipstick.

Neither of them said anything about Grandma's memory problem. Am I supposed to forget about it?

This entire day doesn't seem like it actually happened. Right now it's nine p.m., and I'm lying in bed staring at the ceiling.

Fourteen hours ago I was on my way to Portland.

Seven hours ago PJ and I were hugging.

Two hours ago my uncle who I never knew was my uncle until today gave me his phone number.

I don't know what to feel; there are too many things to have feelings about.

I have homework, which is what I told Grandma I was going to do when I went to my room.

I guess I'm already lying to her again, because I can't make myself do it.

Snufkin hops onto the bed, headbutts my hand, kneads my stomach, settles, purrs.

FIFTEEN

"WHAT'D YOU GET BUSTED FOR?" ENRIQUE asked when I walked into the Youth Council meeting.

"What do you mean?" I think I know.

Yesenia's not here yet. So far it's only Enrique and Faisal sitting on the sunset blanket. I find a spot across from them. Linh is getting out the big plastic toy bins. I'm kind of glad, because cleaning toys doesn't require any thought, but also not glad, because when we're doing something necessary and boring, it means we can talk about other things, and there are whole categories of things I don't want to discuss.

"The security guy was talking to you before," says Enrique. "What were you doing? Boosting anime DVDs from the adult section?"

This is such a specific speculation that it makes me think Enrique has done it himself, or at least thought about it.

I didn't think Alonso was really listening to us, since we haven't officially started the meeting yet and he was looking at his phone, but he jumps in: "You know, just because someone has a job where they need to respond to incidents doesn't mean that's the only reason they'd be having a conversation. Also, don't you think everyone deserves some privacy?"

"No they don't! Not if Alex got busted! Alex never gets in trouble! The world needs to know!" He snort-laughs and nudges Faisal.

"I am actually in trouble right now, for your information," I say. "Youth Council is the only place I'm allowed to go."

Why did I open my mouth? I guess telling Enrique he was wrong somehow outweighed my need to not talk about stuff.

"Whoa! So is the security guy like your parole officer? Like you have to report to him?" Enrique seems totally thrilled.

"Yes," I say all sarcastic, "that's exactly right."

It isn't too far from the truth. Because I lied about going to the library when I took the bus to Portland, the deal now is that I have to prove I actually *am* at the library when I go by checking in with Uncle Dean, who then lets Grandma know I'm legitimately here.

But he and I haven't had a real conversation, about Grandma or anything else.

I don't know how I'd start one, and it seems like he doesn't know, either.

So he's basically still just responding to incidents.

I'm an incident.

And I have zero idea of what his life is outside the library. I mean, is a library security guy what he wanted to be? Did he leave to go to school or anything? Does he know Kyla, since she grew up here? Does he miss my mom? Was he friends with my dad ever?

Yesenia comes in and sits next to me. We've been texting

some, and I told her that me and PJ made up but not how. She didn't seem super curious about it; mostly she wanted to send me videos of the new dances she's learning. Like, she'll send one that's an example of how to do it, and then one of herself doing it, and she'll want me to say if it looks like she's got it, and honestly it's always hard for me to tell? But I try to notice the little details of foot and arm placement and if she's in time with the music.

Alonso asks a check-in question about what animals we would be if we were animals. Linh, it turns out, knows a lot about cassowaries, and how they're the world's most dangerous bird, with claws like daggers, and that a cassowary has literally killed at least one man. She makes a great case that by being a cassowary she'd be not only a bird but also a fashionable supervillain, and that launches us into talking about what other animals are villains, or heroes for that matter, which gets us through half the meeting. Then Yesenia asks what people's favorite foods are for Thanksgiving. I have actually forgotten that Thanksgiving is next week, and that my dad's going to pick me and Grandma up and drive us to Bend.

"Not everyone celebrates Thanksgiving," Alonso reminds us. "So instead, how about we talk about favorite foods for family gatherings?"

Everyone is immediately enthusiastic about this topic, except there's also some complaining about how it's making us too hungry and it's totally unfair that we're not eating all the foods people are talking about at this exact moment.

I can't come up with anything to say. I'm wondering what my mom's favorite food was, and if I would like it.

After Youth Council I go to tell Uncle Dean that I want to stick around for a while to do homework, and to ask if I can get a ride with him after so Grandma won't have to drive in the dark. I'm also asking him because maybe this way he'll have to actually talk to me.

"Um, I don't know, you should probably get yourself home now. She's expecting you." Uncle Dean isn't looking at me. He's looking all the way across the room for some reason, but there isn't any security-guard-needing type of drama happening as far as I can tell. It's just Alonso helping a lady do something on a computer.

"But there's stuff I need that's only here!" I say. "We're supposed to use a primary source for history, and the old Failin newspapers aren't online."

Uncle Dean cracks his knuckles and his wrists and keeps not looking at me. "All right, go find your newspaper. I just need to check on something real quick."

"And you'll call Grandma and tell her? I would, but, you know—"

"Yep," he says. "Yep, I'll do that. How old is old, anyway? Are we talking the eighteen hundreds or the nineties? Never mind, go find your paper."

I know where the old newspapers are from the time PJ and I decided to find out what happened in Failin on the days we were born. (Answer: nothing interesting. But some of the ads were funny.)

It takes a while to find the article I need, and then the copier is messed up, so I have to get someone to fix it—not Alonso; I don't know where he went. By the time it's all sorted out and I have the copy of the article about how Failin celebrated the two hundredth birthday of the United States, the library is closing. I find Uncle Dean by the entrance; Alonso's there, too.

"Oh, do you guys carpool or something?" I ask.

"Or something," says Uncle Dean.

We walk out to the parking lot, and they stop by an old beige Toyota Corolla. Uncle Dean goes to the passenger side. Alonso says, "Are you sure? There's that policy about not transporting minors." As he's unlocking the driver's side, I look for some reason at his hand and see his ring. Hematite.

"I don't think it applies when the minor is a family member," says Uncle Dean.

"You drive, then," says Alonso. They switch places and we all get in.

"You're together," I say.

"Yes," says Alonso.

"We sure are," says Uncle Dean.

Part of me is thrilled to suddenly know two more gay adults. I thought Alonso might be, just from things he's said and books he's recommended, and how he wasn't ever weird about me and PJ being girlfriends. But another part of me feels like a wrecking ball has just demolished the wall between home and not-home.

"When were you planning on telling me?"

Alonso fastens his seat belt with a loud click. "You've already had a lot to take in recently, Alex. We weren't sure if you needed anything else sprung on you right away—"

"What, did you think I wouldn't be able to handle it? I mean,

I'm gay, for your information. Or are you guys like closeted at work?"

Saying I'm gay out loud makes my face heat up and my pulse thud fast but also it's just true, and also Alonso already knows, unless he's way more oblivious than I think he is, and also if Uncle Dean were going to have a problem with it, it would make him the world's most gigantic hypocrite, so whatever. I shut up and wait for my pulse and face to calm down.

The car is super clean, especially considering how old it is, and the only thing in the back seat besides me is a stack of books. There's a small rip in the upholstery. I start worrying at it like a hangnail, and then I can't stop myself from opening my mouth again.

"Also, *Uncle* Dean?" I put extra angry emphasis on *uncle*. "If I hadn't gone to see PJ in Portland and Grandma hadn't showed up at the library, would you have ever even told me who you are, even? Or would you just have kept, like, staring at me from across the library like a creeper?"

The rip in the upholstery is bigger now. There's some kind of crumbly foam underneath. I should stop messing with it. I don't.

"It was hard," says Uncle Dean, "it was hard, to know—to know—"

"How to start," says Alonso.

"Yeah, that," says Uncle Dean.

I've barely noticed that the car has been moving this whole time, that we are, in fact, turning onto Church, two blocks away from my house. I have some crumbly foam under my fingernail. I move the stack of books so it covers the rip.

Uncle Dean parks on the street, by the garbage bin that's still out from this morning.

I wish I could pinpoint when coming home went from feeling good to being something I have to brace myself for.

But then again, what good would it do me to know exactly when it changed?

"Thanks for the ride," I say, and it feels like I should say more, but I don't know what, so I don't.

Uncle Dean and Alonso drive off. I wheel the bin back to its non-trash-day spot by the garage, then stand outside the front door for a little while before I open it.

"Let me see that article you got for school," Grandma says, after I've hung up my coat. I don't know what to be impressed with more: the fact that Uncle Dean told her about my exact assignment, or that she remembered what he told her.

I dig the article out of my backpack and hand it to her. "Oh, my, yes, the bicentennial!" she says. "That was such a day. There was a big to-do about the fireworks, as I recall. They set them off from the top of the brewery, and someone was where they shouldn't have been and got hurt. And I had a red-white-and-blue dress with the Stars and Stripes right on it—oh, it was a neat deal!" Grandma smiles.

"That sounds really pretty, Grandma," I say.

SIXTEEN

GRANDMA, DAD, AND I HAVE BEEN ON THE road for about an hour. Yesenia's already sent me a picture of Snufkin eating, and another of him sitting on her lap. If he likes her better than he likes us by the time we come back, I'll be mad.

I texted Uncle Dean. I don't know why exactly; it just seemed like something I should do.

> my dad's driving me and Grandma to Bend
>
> for Thanksgiving
>
> that's what we usually do

Three dots from Uncle Dean for a while, then:

> Thanks for telling me. Hope you all have a good holiday.

I kind of want to send an eye roll or a gagging gif, but Uncle Dean and I don't know each other like that. Instead I just type:

> hope you and alonso do too

I wonder what they do for Thanksgiving. I don't know if

Alonso has family in Failin. Part of me thinks he must, because why else would he even be in Failin? It's not an exciting place to live. But also I know sometimes people move away from their families because of jobs, so maybe that's why. And if he does have family in Failin, do they like Uncle Dean? Are they okay with them being a couple?

"Looks like we're going to have some nice clear weather for a post-feast hike tomorrow!" Dad says cheerily.

"Oh great!" I say, which is the opposite of what I think. Dad and Laura and Liam and Logan are the kind of outdoorsy people who don't seem to understand that anyone could possibly not be outdoorsy. And Dad's first name is Lucas, so they're also one of those families where everyone's name starts with the same letter, which, I sort of get why you might want to name your kids with the same first letter, like a way of being connected even beyond everyone having the same last name. But when it comes to the adults, it just seems super weird—like, what are the odds? Did you decide you wanted to be with this person because their name started with the same letter as yours?

When my dad was with my mom, it was Lucas and Joan.

Or Joanie, I guess she got called both.

Anyway, different letters.

Was my mom outdoorsy?

If she wasn't, what did they do instead?

I know they met when they were both working at a restaurant.

Maybe they liked cooking together?

It's not that I've never thought about these things before. It's just that now that the giant fact of Uncle Dean existing is suddenly part of my reality, it's harder to pretend that everything that happened before I was born doesn't affect me.

Now Dad is asking me about school in the way he has where he doesn't really know what I'm studying or what's important to me (which are often different), and I think he's basing his questions on the twins' school, which makes sense, but also they're younger and do basically every sport, so as far as I can tell, they think of school as the thing they have to sit through before all the sports can start again. I'm answering him and also sending PJ pictures of otters holding hands.

"Hey, don't be on that phone too much, honey—you have the rest of your life to be tethered to devices. Enjoy your freedom while you can," Dad says. Then his phone pipes up to tell him the next turn he has to make.

"I don't see why you need that robot telling you what to do," says Grandma. She has said this, or something really close to it, seven times so far, each time Dad's phone has given him an instruction.

I tell myself that I'm getting carsick, which does sometimes happen, especially when I try to read, which is unfair, because it seems like a long car ride should be the perfect time to read. But I know that the heaviness behind my eyes, and how the air has turned to glue that I can't get enough of into my lungs, and how I feel like I might throw up, has nothing to do with being in the car or Dad's driving.

PJ texts me what I now recognize as the view through her bedroom window, mostly her neighbors' roof plus some trees and phone poles. The neighbors have just put up their Christmas lights. Besides the usual cute animals and hearts and long conversations, we've gotten into this thing where every so often we send each other pictures of what we're seeing at that moment, so we can feel more like we're in the same place. I get a quick jolt of good feeling, put my phone against the minivan window, and send my view to her. I do like this part of the drive when the landscape changes, going from rhododendrons and dogwoods to junipers and sage, and the air starts to smell different and feel dry. It is, objectively, really pretty.

But the closer we get to Dad and Laura's, and the more times Grandma says the same thing and Dad responds like it isn't now the seventeenth time she's told him he shouldn't need a robot telling him what to do, the harder it is for me not to wish that the phone would just transport me, and I'd be with PJ in her room, and we could hold hands like the otters.

DAD AND LAURA ALREADY HAVE THEIR

Christmas lights up, plus an inflatable snowman, except it's not inflated right now so it just looks melted. I always forget how big their house is until we're pulling into the long gravel driveway, which has an arch over it that says WELCOME TO LARCH RANCH. (Another *L*.) Larch is a kind of tree, and there are in fact a lot of larches on their property, which I know because I asked Dad about it once and he pointed them out, but it is not an actual ranch.

Liam and Logan are playing soccer in the driveway. Dad honks at them, and they get out of the way. They look like they resent both having to stop for even as long as it takes for Dad to park and the fact that Grandma and I are here. I don't really blame them; when we're here, things are less fun for them, pretty much by definition.

Dad and Laura have told them to call Grandma "Aunt Kathy," which doesn't make any sense. I mean, obviously she isn't their grandma so that's not what they should call her, but also she's not their aunt? I guess the idea is that they should think of Grandma as being part of their family, too, but Laura has two actual sisters, so Liam and Logan have real aunts, so again, using *aunt* for her is just weird.

Anyway, knowing all this doesn't make me like Liam and Logan any better.

I'm stepping down from the minivan to the ground when the soccer ball hits me in the knee. I don't know which of them kicked it. I know it's a cliché with twins, but I actually can't tell them apart a lot of the time.

"Ow!" I shouldn't have said anything, but I couldn't help it—it hurt.

"Hey hey hey, boys, settle it down! Help Alex and Aunt Kathy with their bags." Laura has come out to greet us. She's one of those strong wiry ladies, like the word *toned* was invented to describe her. She always looks like she could be in an ad for fancy granola: She wears clothes made out of that clingy sporty performance fabric stuff, and she doesn't wear a lot of makeup, but there's always a polished quality to her face, and her nails are always French manicured. They'd look good in the close-up of her holding the bowl of granola.

"So glad you're here, sweetheart!" she says as she hugs me. I wish she wouldn't hug me, partly because her body is much smaller than mine, and also I just don't feel like I know her well enough.

"Well, that was a big drive," says Grandma. "If you'll all excuse me, I believe I'll take a little rest."

Laura lets go of me and takes Grandma's arm, which is not necessary—Grandma doesn't have any trouble walking—and leads her inside. I grab my backpack and little wheelie bag—I don't want Liam or Logan to carry it—and follow them. I wish I could get away with taking a nap, too, but when we're here, I sleep on the foldout couch in the living room because Grandma gets the guest room.

"I've got a surprise for you, Alex!" Laura says after Grandma is settled in her room. "We redid my old office as another bedroom! So you'll be in here this time!" She opens the door to the room next to the guest room. The walls are pale pink. There are flowered curtains at the windows and a matching floral duvet on the bed, two teal nightstands that also match, with matching white lamps on them, and a teal dresser with bright yellow knobs. I bet Laura painted the nightstands and dresser herself. I know she likes that kind of thing, because their house is always full of the kind of magazines that are half instructions for do-it-yourself projects and half ads for all the things you're supposed to buy so you can do them.

"Oh wow! This is great!" I say.

"The guys thought I went a little overboard on the girly in here, but come on, when else do I get the chance, right? I'm so glad you like it."

What I like is mostly the fact of the door and its thrilling capacity to be closed, but I nod. "Actually, I'd kind of like to take a nap, too, if that's okay? And I need to charge my phone."

"Of course," Laura says. "Make yourself at home."

"DINNER IS LIGHT TONIGHT, SO WE CAN save room for the feast tomorrow," Laura announces as she puts down a big salad bowl. There was already a plate of carrots, celery, green peppers, and olives, so I suppose I should be glad there's even salad. I like salad, and Laura makes good ones, but I don't think "saving room" is an actual thing.

"Lame!" says Liam or Logan, which is something you shouldn't ever say because it's ableist against people who have mobility limitations, but if I tried telling them that, it would not go well. "Yeah!" says Logan or Liam. "We're growing athletes—we need protein even if some people don't!"

"Everyone needs protein, boys. Protein and carbs, and even fats!" says Laura. "There are walnuts in the salad, and smoked salmon. A little goat cheese, too!"

"It'll be delicious," says my dad.

It is, but there isn't enough of it. Even if I wanted to ask for seconds, which is not something I like doing when I'm in this house, there wouldn't have been any seconds to have.

After dinner Grandma excuses herself, and I want to, too, but I don't. The rest of us watch a soccer game where most of the time I'm worrying that the players are going to get injured, and then one of them does, something with his knee. It makes my own knee feel sore again to see it.

Laura asks me to help her load the dishwasher, so of course I do. "We're so glad to have you here," she says. "Failin is too far away! And there are a lot of things around here we never have time for on these short visits. I'd love to take you to the High Desert Museum. I just saw they have a new baby porcupine! Tell you what, tomorrow? Let's go out in the morning, just the two of us."

"Won't you have—I mean, isn't there a lot of cooking stuff to do?" I know it's sexist to assume Laura will be the one cooking everything, but that's how it's always been before when we've come.

"I decided to take the pressure off this year. I prepped a lot in advance, and it's a smoked turkey so it just needs heating up." Laura rinses the big salad bowl and puts it in the drying rack. I scrape the walnuts Liam or Logan has left on their plate into the compost bucket.

"Oh," I say. "Are your sisters and everyone coming?"

Laura's the oldest of three sisters. She's also older than my dad. Two years ago at Thanksgiving, her sister Becca made what she called a signature drink that all the adults but Grandma had a lot of, and her other sister Cassie kept teasing Laura about being a cougar. At first it seemed like Laura didn't mind; she even put her hands out like claws and made a *rowr* sound at my dad, which I immediately wished I could unsee and unhear. But then after a while she left the living room and didn't come back.

"Not this year," Laura says. "It'll be just us." She squeezes my shoulder.

"Won't the museum be closed, though? Because of the holiday?"

Laura looks as though that had not occurred to her whatsoever. "Oh, you might be right about that. Well, we'll go for a drive, anyway! Get some girl time in!"

First she wanted me to see a baby porcupine (which actually sounded good) and now it's "girl time"? Maybe she wants to give me a makeover, or there's a diet she wants to tell me about. Or she wants to go on a hike. It could always be a hike.

"Okay, thanks," I say, because what else am I going to say.

SEVENTEEN

EVEN IN THE NEW GUEST ROOM WITH THE door I could close, it was hard to get to sleep. I wondered for a while how come Laura decided she doesn't need an office anymore. And I could hear Grandma moving around in the next room, and there were other sounds, little thunks and mechanical whirs—maybe the furnace or something, just irregular enough not to be able to get used to. Also I kept worrying I was going to bleed on the pink sheets, so I kept checking my pad a million times, and being glad that I was wearing thick sweatpants.

I send PJ pictures of the matching floral curtains and comforter and the extremely teal dresser, and tell her how Laura and I are apparently going somewhere by ourselves first thing tomorrow.

> maybe she wants to get you a dress that also matches, so you'll really go with the room

> ha! maybe

I don't tell her what I actually think is going to happen, which is that Laura will take me on some monster hike so that in her mind I'll somewhat deserve to eat Thanksgiving dinner. My elite swimmer girlfriend has never dealt with anyone who feels like it's their job to make her exercise more. Except for all her coaches, I guess, but in that case it is their job, and also she signed up for it.

> how about you? is it going to be just you and your moms for dinner?

we're going to this friend of mama's who I guess always has a big gathering?

it's called Family Dinner but it isn't anyone's like biological family

pretty sure both my moms have dated some of the other guests also

so it could be Interesting

> that sounds like it'll be very different from the day I'm going to have

yeah, probably!

WHEN WE GET IN THE CAR I ASSUME LAURA'S

going to drive us to a trailhead, but instead she drives us into town and even takes us to a Starbucks drive-through to get a skinny half-caf latte for her and a hot chocolate for me. The hot chocolate is good, but I'm suspicious of it. It feels like a bribe, and I don't know what I'm being bribed to do, or not do.

"So, Alex, I'm sorry we can't do the museum today. We'll have to make that happen another time, but there is a place I want to show you—we'll actually all be going there later; we have a tour scheduled—but I wanted to show you now with just us. It's really beautiful, and they do such a great job— Oh, but I'm getting ahead of myself. Honey, you know how much we love your grandma, right? And we've respected how she's wanted you to live with her over the years."

I stare out the window. We're going by a used car dealership with one of those creepy moving figures out front with the grin and the spiky "hair." PJ and I both find them terrifying, so of course we had to look them up online. They're called Wind Dancers and they are patented, we learned—the dancers themselves and also how they work. The patent is for an "apparatus and method for providing inflated undulating figures." As though inflated undulating figures were, like, a big unmet need in the community.

Laura goes on. "And you know, we've just been thinking: We're coming to a time when your grandma might be needing some more help, and she also might enjoy the company of more people her own age."

"I help her," I say. I don't know about the "people her own age" part. Most of the book club people are younger, I think, and book club is her favorite thing.

"Honey, of course you help her!" Laura pats me on the knee. "But no one expects you to be able to help her with all the things that might be getting more challenging for her these days."

I remember the dementia websites. *The activities of daily living.* Is she going to get so she can't dress or bathe herself? Will she need to wear diapers? I can put Tiger Balm on her back and neck, but I can't imagine, like, helping her shower or changing her diaper. Or actually I can, and it's gross and embarrassing and sad. What I can't imagine is her letting me, or being anything but furious at the idea.

I don't want any of that to happen. Maybe it won't.

Laura's pulling into a parking lot. The sign says LURIE MANOR: ASSISTED LIVING SENIOR RESIDENCES.

My hot chocolate has gone cold.

"See how beautifully they decorate? And the residents help!"

There's a scarecrow and a truly enormous pile of pumpkins next to the Lurie Manor sign. The scarecrow is holding a HAPPY THANKSGIVING banner.

I decide it's the Pumpkin Palace.

"That's a lot of pumpkins," I say. "Does Grandma know you want her to live here?" I think I sound calmer than I feel.

"Your dad's talking to her now."

"Okay," I say. How come he's not talking to me? "Can we go back to the house? I have to change my tampon, and I forgot to bring more." This sounds like an excuse but is actually true: I felt the splorch of a big clot of blood just now, and I hope I won't bleed through my underwear.

"Of course," says Laura. "But while we're on the way, while it's just us, will you tell me honestly what you think, how you're feeling about this?"

"I think Grandma won't like it."

Laura screws up her mouth in a weird way. "Well, I know it'll be a big change for her, a big adjustment, but I'm asking you about you."

I can tell how much she wants me to say something positive. It hurts to stay quiet, with Laura practically vibrating with wanting me to tell her—I don't know—that secretly I've always wanted to live with them? That this is totally the right thing for Grandma and I'm so grateful they thought of it? That I can't wait to play sports with Liam and Logan? I keep not saying anything. I sip my cold hot chocolate and get to a sludgy part. I let the sweet sludge melt slowly in my mouth before I swallow.

"It's a lot," says Laura, filling the silence. "I know. It's a lot to take in. That's why I wanted to give you this time to start getting used to the idea."

So according to their plan, I have to take in the idea, and Pumpkin Palace has to take in Grandma, and Dad and Laura have to take in me. Like a stray cat. Which makes me think of Snufkin. I bet the Pumpkin Palace doesn't allow pets. I bet Liam and Logan don't like cats.

"Thank you for showing me the place," I say.

I stay quiet after that. After a while Laura puts on a playlist of soft instrumental music and hums along. She has a nice voice. She's nice. I don't want to live with her.

"GOOD MORNING, LIAM," SAYS LAURA.

"Hey," says Liam. He's got the refrigerator open, pouring himself a big glass of juice.

I try to find differences between him and his brother. He's done something with his hair—gel, I think? or maybe it's just greasy—that makes it a different shape from Logan's, and his voice is a little softer. "You should come watch us and then play. You'd like this game. It's pretty funny to watch, too—I'm not even joking," he says to me, and because that sounds better than the other things I was thinking of doing, those being either helping Laura with the Thanksgiving cooking while being sad, or staring at my phone while being sad, I follow Liam to the living room, where Logan already has the game loaded. It's a game where you're a horrible goose, and you go places you're not supposed to be and steal stuff and just be generally bothersome to the humans, and it is, objectively, supremely hilarious.

THANKSGIVING DINNER, WHICH IS MORE like Thanksgiving late lunch, is buffet style. Laura bought a lot of things from the fancy grocery, basically all the side dishes except the bread-and-celery-and-onion stuffing that Grandma always makes and the gravy that's Dad's specialty. (He once told me he'd learned to make it back when he was working at the restaurant where he met my mom. I think about that every time we have it.) Everyone takes their plates to the living room, because there's an important football game to watch. I get the feeling it's also because TV is easier than talking. I wonder how Dad's talk with Grandma went. She's been pretty quiet, too, since Laura and I got back.

Another good thing about the buffet-style Thanksgiving is that no one's paying as much attention to how much food anyone else is eating as I was expecting. For once I get as much gravy as I want, so the turkey is actually good and not dry. The team Liam and Logan and Dad were rooting for wins, and it puts them all in a good mood. Liam and Logan even do the dishes, by which

I mean putting them in the dishwasher, but it's still kind of a miracle as far as I'm concerned.

I text PJ:

> how is Family Dinner so far

> there's a lot of wine happening

> steph has some really funny old photos of mama

> with like a very self-inflicted-looking haircut

> but there isn't anyone my age so overall it's pretty boring

> how's yours going?

"Hey, let's take that drive we talked about earlier, eh?" Dad says.

> ok so far

> but i think it's about to not be

"THAT'S A LOT OF PUMPKINS," GRANDMA

says, and it makes me laugh, because it's exactly what I said, too.

"It sure is!" I say.

Then Liam and Logan laugh, and one of them repeats "It shore is!" in a goofy accent, which is, I guess, the way they think I sound.

There's old music playing over some kind of sound system as we all go inside. Old like really old, like from when Grandma was young, which is the point of it, I suppose, but it's not the kind of music she likes. For a minute I wish the sound system was playing "Mole in the Ground" so she could sing along, but I don't think she'd be in the mood. The first thing we see is a giant aquarium, the kind that takes up an entire wall. The fish swimming back and forth are really pretty, and I'd be happy to watch them for a long time, but then a long-haired blond woman comes up and says, "Happy Thanksgiving! You must be the Tollefsons! And Mrs. Eager, am I right? I'm Tiffany, and I get to show you all around the manor!"

Ugh, they actually call it a *manor*.

Tiffany shakes hands with Dad and then with Grandma, and leads us past the aquarium. "This is our coffee shop—we've always got some goodies here—and as you can see, people like to gather and play cards, or maybe read some magazines." Tiffany waves at a card-playing group, then at a magazine reader. "You all want some coffee or tea? How about a cookie?"

"Yeah!" Liam and Logan get chocolate chip cookies. So does Grandma. She gets coffee, too. I don't get anything—part of me feels like the Pumpkin Palace is like those places in stories where if you eat the food, you'll be trapped there. Also, I'm not hungry.

Once Grandma has her cookie and coffee, she sits down at one of the little tables. "Want to rest a bit?" asks Tiffany. "We can certainly do that. But I'm excited for you to see the movie theater and the pub, and to tell you about our activities and dining! We've got a feast happening today, of course. But the food is always real good; I always say I'd eat here even if I didn't work here!"

"You all go on ahead," says Grandma. I sit down in the chair opposite her.

"Okay!" says Tiffany. "You just make yourself comfortable, and we'll come back for you after you catch your breath a bit, sound good?"

"You go on ahead," Grandma says again.

Laura and Dad look worried. Tiffany takes Laura's arm and says quietly, but I can still hear, "It's all right. We see it a lot, this type of resistance; we find it's better to go with it and not force anything."

They wander away.

Grandma takes a bite of her cookie, then a sip of her coffee. "Well, we'd best be getting home now," she says. "Do you remember where we parked? Joanie, where'd we leave the car?"

"I'm not sure," I say, and I hate that my voice is a little shaky, but I can't help it. "Maybe we could stay a little longer? I kind of want a cookie," I lie. "Do you want another one?"

The problem is our car is in Failin.

The problem is I can't drive.

The problem is I can't fix anything.

Yesenia sent a photo of Snufkin, curled up on the blanket that's the same gray color as him. *Camouflaged!* she's captioned it. I send back a smile emoji. "Look at Snufkin," I say, holding up my phone to Grandma.

"Camouflaged," she says, and there's a moment where I'm surprised she and Yesenia had the same take, and then I realize it's just that Grandma has read her caption.

A Pumpkin Palace person comes up to us in a scooter. It's a pretty tricked-out scooter, with a bright blue tray to put snacks and books on, and a hook for hanging a bag from, so it's easy to reach. "Got your grandkid visiting, huh?" they ask. "That's nice. Nice day for it. Heck, any day's a nice day for it, right?"

Grandma smiles. "Alex actually lives with me. We're both just visiting," she says. Then she stands up. "And we need to get a move on. Nice chatting with you!"

Grandma heads for the exit. I follow her and tug on her sleeve when we get to the aquarium wall. "I think we're supposed to wait?" I ask. "For Dad and Laura and the twins?" Since she used my right name again just now, I'm hoping she got unconfused. "And I really like these fish—maybe we can watch them for a while. While we wait?"

"This isn't going to work," Grandma says. She's not talking to me, though, she's talking to Dad and Laura and Tiffany, who have all, suddenly, reappeared. I don't know what happened to Liam and Logan. Maybe they're getting more cookies.

"I wish you'd give it a chance," says Dad. "It's so convenient—"

"Too convenient," says Grandma. "Come along, Alex." And she walks out.

> did you know my dad and stepmom want to put grandma in an assisted living facility

> this one

I send Uncle Dean a photo of the sign with the scarecrow and the pumpkins. I honestly don't know if he and my dad even talk to each other, or if he and Alonso had any idea this was happening.

There's no reply right away, which I hate. I guess he might not have his phone on him. But it seems like since he gave me his number, he should have been expecting that I would use it. I type some more:

> she really doesn't want to live there
>
> can you do something

EIGHTEEN

WHEN MY PHONE RANG, I ALMOST DIDN'T pick it up because I'm used to Grandma being the only person to call me ever and she's right next to me, standing by Dad and Laura's minivan waiting for them to come out of the Pumpkin Palace. They're probably looking for Liam and Logan. I wonder if the Pumpkin Palace has a video game room.

"Alex, hey, we're both here. We have you on speaker," says Alonso when I finally answer.

"Hi, Alex. Happy Thanksgiving," says Uncle Dean. I've almost forgotten it's still Thanksgiving. "Got your text and just wanted to see how things were going."

"Will you talk to my dad and Laura?" It's the only thing I can think of.

"Who are you speaking to, Alex?" Grandma asks.

"Uncle Dean," I say. I don't know if she knows about Alonso.

"Let me speak with him, please," she says.

"Uh, okay," I say, and hand my phone to her.

"Dean? Yes, hello. Happy Thanksgiving. Alex and I need to get back home. I don't have the car, so you'd best come get us."

THESE MIGHT BE THE LONGEST HOURS OF my life so far. We rode back to Dad and Laura's in total silence; even Liam and Logan stayed quiet for some reason. Then Grandma packed her things, so I did, too, and now she and I are sitting in the living room waiting for Uncle Dean to get here. And Alonso? I hope so, but I also don't hope so, in case Grandma doesn't like him? Or, I don't know, in case something else bad happens? What if they get in a car accident on the way because Uncle Dean's driving too fast?

Funny, he's totally become Uncle Dean in my head now, not the Creeper. I think about how strange it must have been for him, seeing his niece at his work for so long but not feeling like he could talk to her.

I wonder if I remind him of my mom.

And I wonder what it feels like to be Grandma now. Is it like those kinds of dreams where you think you understand how everything works, and then suddenly you're somewhere else you don't recognize, with different people you don't know, and when they talk to you, you can't make sense of what they're saying?

It makes me too sad to keep thinking about that, so I just lean closer to Grandma on the big squishy leather sofa, feeling her familiar solidness and warmth.

Dad and Laura are upstairs arguing. I can't hear exactly what they're saying, but it's obvious it's about us. Liam and Logan must still be in their rooms. I'm sure this is all super weird for them, too.

I want to text PJ, but I don't know what to say. Instead I text Yesenia:

> we might be home sooner than we told you
>
> like late tonight

Three dots, then she writes back:

> what's up???

it's complicated, I type.
Then I delete that and type *stuff*.
Then I delete that and type:

> Grandma's mad at my dad
>
> ooh family drama!!!!
>
> yeah
>
> that's holidays for ya

And somehow it's reading that word—*holidays*—that turns the tight clenched-up feeling in my stomach into something hotter that makes it all the way up to my head, and I can't sit still anymore waiting next to Grandma; I'm not even sure I can stay in this house.

Liam and Logan come in and turn on the TV to another football game.

I scream, "TURN THAT OFF!"

"You don't even live here! You can't tell us what to do!" says Liam or Logan.

Then Dad and Laura are in the room, too, and Laura's saying,

"Gosh, sounds like some people here are hungry, or what is it they say these days—hangry? Hungry and angry?"

"WHY ARE YOU PRETENDING THIS IS ABOUT FOOD?" I don't wait for anyone to answer; I run out, out of the living room, down the long hallway with the cubbies where they store all Liam and Logan's gear—even if I did want to move in with them, I'd have to be in Laura's ex-office-now-girly-room and keep pretending I liked it, and besides, Dad didn't even care enough to talk to me about moving in with them himself; he offloaded it onto Laura, and I bet he offloaded the stuff about Grandma, too; I bet Laura was the one who found the Pumpkin Palace and set up the tour of the manor with Tiffany, and now Laura's still trying to hold everyone together, but I don't want to *be* together, not with them.

I feel bad about running out on Grandma, but what's happening with her is too big, and I couldn't be in there anymore, I just couldn't. It's cold and windy, and that feels *bracing*, a Grandma word. The bracing cold air makes my dumb hot face feel less like it's actually on fire. It's dark, too, and that's also good; if anyone else is out walking for some reason, I don't want them to see me crying.

I rub my eyes and sniff snot back into my nose, then wipe it with the back of my hand. There's a lot of space between the houses on this street, and they're set a long way back from the road, and I'm glad about that, too, because again, I don't want anyone to see me, especially if that anyone was having some kind of actually wholesome celebration with a family who actually talk to each other about things that actually matter.

I've come up to a big flat rock, halfway as tall as me and maybe six feet across. It's on someone's property, sure, but first of all it seems stupid to think that anyone could literally own a rock, because a rock is obviously part of nature, and second of all I just really want to hoist myself up and lie down on it, so that's what I do.

It's a clear night with lots of stars. I think of the star-watching rock from Madeleine L'Engle books, and for a minute I wish that being here on this rock, looking up at stars, would turn me into Meg Murry, who, sure, went through a lot, but had a really great family.

But Meg didn't have PJ.

I think again about texting her, but I still don't know what to say. I wish she could just magically know everything that's been happening.

I aim my phone at the sky and send her stars.

I've been lying on the rock for a while, getting colder but not wanting to move, when I hear someone's footsteps on the gravel and see a wavering circle of light from their phone.

It's whoever's property this is, probably, here to tell me it's against the law for me to lie on their rock. Or maybe it's Dad.

"Alex?"

Not Dad. Alonso.

I sit up and squint at him.

"So you came because my dad couldn't be bothered?"

Part of me is glad he's here, but too much of me is still too mad for me to tell him that.

"That rock is cool," says Alonso. "You found a good spot."

I'm mad at how gentle Alonso's voice is. Like he took a class in Talking to Troubled Teens.

"So the plan is we're going to head out pretty soon here," he says, and yawns gigantically.

"Did they even care I was gone?"

I didn't mean to say that out loud.

I slide off the rock, but stay leaning against it.

"They definitely did. Look, just because we're adults doesn't mean we have everything figured out."

"That's obvious," I say.

"Honestly," Alonso says, "everyone was wanting to go look for you, to take the car and do it that way, but I volunteered because, well, they still all had a lot to say to each other."

"And if you were out here looking for me, you wouldn't have to be in there with them to hear it."

"Exactly."

I can't see Alonso's face clearly since it's so dark. He's one more person whose life is really changing because of Grandma. And I guess maybe it'll change also if the library-losing-funding thing happens, which I feel bad for not really having thought about for a while, but well, I just haven't.

"Did you have to leave— I mean, were you guys at, like, a family thing?" I ask.

"We're not big on this particular holiday. Don't get me wrong—we did have to leave right before a really good part of the movie we were watching, but, you know, we'll cope."

"Thanks. I mean, I'm glad you guys came. I just didn't really know what to do."

"Yeah," says Alonso, "there's a lot of that going around."

NINETEEN

WHEN ALONSO AND I GOT BACK TO THE house, it was just Laura, my dad, and Uncle Dean in the living room. Dad was pacing, arms folded across his chest. Uncle Dean was holding a mug in both hands, sitting in the armchair where Dad usually sits, looking uncomfortable. Laura was scooched up at one corner of the sofa like she was being crowded by invisible people.

"Is Grandma already in the car? I thought we were leaving, like, right now?" I ask, not sure exactly who I'm asking.

"*Shhhh*, keep your voice down, Alex," says Laura. "Your grandma was very tired. I managed to convince her to go to bed—you all can still leave in the morning, of course, and this way you won't have to drive in the dark."

Alonso goes over to Uncle Dean, and for one second I think he's going to sit on his lap, but he just leans against the back of the armchair, puts a hand on Uncle Dean's shoulder, and squeezes briefly. I feel like it's meant to be an apology and a support at the same time, like he wants Uncle Dean to know he's there for him, and he's also sorry he wasn't with him before, when he was out looking for me.

I think of Laura taking me on the trip to the Pumpkin Palace this morning. (How was it only this morning? This day is a million years long.) I wonder why it's the people who aren't related to me—Alonso and Laura—who are making the biggest efforts.

"That doesn't make any sense. She really wanted to get out of here, and I don't blame her," I say, looking at Dad.

The wind is loud outside. Branches thwack against the windows.

"Your grandmother is having a hard time with the idea that she needs help," Dad says.

Would he have said anything if I hadn't been looking at him?

When I lied about having to study all day at the library, when I was actually going to Portland, Grandma said she knew I didn't think I should ever have to ask for help, and how it was better to ask than to struggle on your own.

I guess she thought that was true for me but not for her.

I feel awful and ashamed about that lie all over again, but what I say is "She doesn't *want* help! She wants to be the one helping! It's like you don't even know her!"

I stalk out to the kitchen just as Uncle Dean says, "Maybe we don't. 'Cause that sure hasn't always been the case."

I want to ask him what Grandma was like when he and my mom were growing up, except I also don't want to. I'm mad and sad that I don't already know, and also I'm scared that whatever he'd say would change my whole idea of who she is.

More than it's changing already, I mean.

My throat's dry. I grab a glass. A bottle of Excedrin PM is next to the tea bags. Did Laura actually drug Grandma so she'd go to sleep and they could all talk about her behind her back? I take a picture of the bottle with my phone, like it's evidence, and that makes me think of watching mysteries with Grandma and her always knowing who did it, sometimes even before they did it, and I want to cry again. Instead I fill the glass from the tap, drink the water, refill the glass, and come back into the living room, where no one is talking and they all look like they want to be somewhere else.

"You know what you should do? Say you lost your job or something and you need somewhere to stay," I tell Uncle Dean. "She'd let you move in, and she could feel like she was doing you a big favor, and then you'd be there, and you could see what she needs help with, because apparently no one thinks I can do anything! And if we're really not leaving tonight, I'm going to bed."

Laura is sitting near where my wheelie bag is, and when I come to get it, she reaches out for my hand.

"Honey, honey, of course we think you can do things; we just don't think you need to be doing them by yourself!"

"Unlike the way you've been making decisions about my mother," says Uncle Dean. It's the first time I've heard him say straight out that Grandma is his mom.

"Oh, excuse us for not consulting you!" says my dad. "When you've been so present in her life! As though you didn't spin out completely when—"

"We're not having that conversation, Lucas." Uncle Dean cuts Dad off. "We're talking about now."

My throat is dry again, even though I drank all that water.

Also, I need to pee, and to take out my tampon, and so much happened before I was even born, a mountain of things.

But it's a mountain of *hidden* things, things that never get talked about, and suddenly in my head I'm hearing the version of Grandma's favorite song that has a different title, not *Mole* in the Ground, but *Hole: If I was a hole in the ground / I'd be a mountain upside down / Wish I was a hole in the ground.*

A hole. Like you dig to bury someone.

I think I want to know everything, but do I really?

"Just tell me, how much does that place cost per month?" Uncle Dean asks.

"Now, you don't need to worry about that. We're prepared to handle—" Laura says, and Uncle Dean interrupts again, "Well, maybe *I'm* not prepared to handle you handling it!"

"These places usually have waiting lists, as I understand it," says Alonso in his Talking to Troubled Teens voice. I'm glad he uses it on grown-ups, too. "So maybe this isn't something we need to settle tonight?"

"I'm sorry, do you think *you're* involved in this decision?" Dad asks. That makes me catch fire but at the same time feel bitingly cold, and again, I can't be in the room with any of them anymore.

Down the hall to the bathroom, dragging my wheelie bag, absurdly, like it's a pet on a weird leash. Locking the bathroom door. Taking the tampon out. A drop of blood from the tampon splashes on the white tile, and I stare at it for a while as I pee. Then I clean up the drop, wrap the tampon in toilet paper, throw it out, find a pad, attach it to my underwear. Think about staying in the bathroom all night but decide that someone will need it before morning. So instead I unlock the door, go down the hall, carefully open the door to the room where Grandma's sleeping, take off my shoes, and crawl in bed next to her. She's snoring, and I don't know if it's because Laura drugged her tea (but wouldn't she have tasted it?) or because she was actually tired, but what matters to me right now is just being near her, the person everyone seemingly wants to help but no one wants to actually talk to.

TWENTY

I WOKE UP IN THE MIDDLE OF THE NIGHT confused about where I was. Then I thought Grandma might be confused, too, if I were there when she woke up, so I crawled out and quietly went back to Laura's ex-office. And then, because I was awake, I texted PJ.

> uncle dean and alonso came to my dad's
>
> not because they were invited
>
> because i texted them
>
> and then they called
>
> and Grandma asked them to come
>
> because dad and laura want to put grandma in assisted living
>
> but she doesn't want to be there
>
> and I don't want her there
>
> and I definitely don't want to live here

> which I would have to if grandma was in the assisted living place

> which had, like, way too many pumpkins outside, see?

I send the picture of the Pumpkin Palace sign, then:

> and everyone's fighting

I wouldn't have sent all this if I wasn't pretty sure that PJ would be asleep. Because I want her to know all of it, but I can't deal with the idea of her reacting to it yet. Like we're barely used to her being in Portland and me being related to Uncle Dean. Which reminded me:

> . . . uncle dean and alonso are a couple btw, did i tell you already?

> also they aren't fighting with each other, just with my dad

> actually it's uncle dean and my dad mostly who are fighting

> and alonso and laura are like caught in the middle

> i mean i am too

> obviously

hey

hi

wow

ouch

i'm sorry

that all sounds super super rough

and you're right that's definitely too many pumpkins

wait

your uncle and ALONSO???

wow

did I tell you I asked mama about him?

your uncle I mean not Alonso

I was wondering if they knew each other growing up

and your mom too

she said it's a small town

so then I asked if she knew what happened with him and your grandma, why they weren't talking for so long

she said she didn't really know

and it wasn't her story to tell

which seemed kind of contradictory

but I didn't push it

. . . anyway, i liked that sky

where was it, your dad's yard?

> no
>
> it was just like down the street
>
> there was a rock i was lying on, a big flat one
>
> that's why the angle was good
>
> how did family dinner turn out

well

pretty sure both my moms are gonna be hungover

so that's excellent

super looking forward to being very quiet with whichever of them gets stuck with driving me to the pool

> . . . how come you're awake?

you texted

i kept my notifications on in case

> thank you

of course

hey

also

i think we're visiting my grandparents for xmas

i mean at least me and kyla are

rachel might have to work

> ANYWAY
>
> the point is that if we're in failin OBVIOUSLY i get to see you
>
> so that's something

> !!!
>
> it sure is

I send a string of hearts.

I WAKE UP AS DISORIENTED AS I WAS worrying Grandma would be. The extremely teal dresser reminds me where I am, and then I look at the clock on my phone and panic: It's past nine already, and we were supposed to leave last night. Everyone is probably mad at me for being so lazy.

I think about just putting new clothes on so I'll be ready quicker, but if I don't shower I'll feel disgusting all day, so I grab black jeans, blue T-shirt, underwear, soft sports bra, deodorant, black socks, soft navy blue hoodie. Ball up the bra and underwear and deodorant and hide them inside the hoodie in case I run into anyone on the way to the bathroom. Pick up the towel and washcloth Laura left on the extremely teal dresser for me. I wish they weren't white. What if I get something gross on them?

I make it to the bathroom without running into anyone, which objectively is not difficult—it's just down the hall from where I was sleeping—but it's a huge relief to set down my bundle of clothes and towel and washcloth and lock the door behind myself.

Dad and Laura have a really good shower, with so much water pressure it almost stings. It does feel better to be clean, and with a fresh tampon. I mean, obviously with a fresh tampon—you'd never use a not-fresh tampon, blech. Anyway, I feel like I'm prepared, kind of, though I'm not sure for what.

I find Grandma sitting on the couch where Laura was last night. She's got her suitcase next to her, so she's definitely ready to go, but she's also reading a magazine. (Dad and Laura don't really have books.) "Good grief, look at this," she says. "They want you to hang tools on the wall and call it decoration!"

I sit down next to her, and she points at a picture of someone's very fancy living room that has a big wooden ruler and an old hammer and a rusty wrench, all mounted on the wall.

"Ha! That's pretty funny," I say. "But I've seen stuff like it at the antique mall, so I guess people must like it?"

"What do they do when they need a hammer, that's what I want to know," says Grandma.

"Did you sleep okay?" I ask.

It's not what I want to know, exactly, but it's the question I can make myself ask.

"Oh, fine," she says. "I'd like to get a move on, but Laura wanted everyone to have breakfast together before we head out, and she seemed to think she needed to pick up some things even though that fridge is packed full."

But how is Grandma actually feeling? Is she still mad about the Pumpkin Palace? Did she forget about it? Where are Uncle Dean and Alonso and Dad and Liam and Logan?

"The rest of them are all out," she says, as though she can read my mind, even as she's supposedly losing hers. "Your dad wanted to roust you out, too, but I said you needed your rest."

"Oh, thanks," I say. It was hard to get to sleep after texting with PJ. I scrolled through random things for a long time afterward.

For a while we just sit and look at the magazine together. Some of the pictures are interesting, but it makes me antsy. Like why is she so calm now?

Just as I'm feeling like I might actually explode, there's a knock at the door, and I rush to answer. It's Uncle Dean and Alonso, and I have a moment of feeling weird that I'm letting them into a house that isn't mine, but then again I guess maybe it sort of is? At least that's what it seemed like Laura was saying, and wanting, when she made a room for me.

And then the van pulls up, and Laura and Dad and Liam and Logan get out with bags from a bagel place and they all come in.

Then Logan says, looking at Alonso, "Did you hire new lawn people?"

He and Liam were already in their rooms last night just doing whatever they do, probably gaming, when Uncle Dean and Alonso got here. I would have been curious about the noise. I guess they weren't, or maybe they had headphones on and didn't hear.

It's weird that they didn't see Uncle Dean and Alonso before they left the house, though. Maybe Uncle Dean and Alonso got up extra early to take a walk or something? I wonder where they slept, and if they slept together, which presumably is what they usually do, but maybe they wouldn't in someone else's house? Then I blush, even though I was literally only thinking about them sleeping, not anything else.

"This is Alex's uncle and his partner, and you're being extremely rude," Laura says, blushing, too.

"Sorry, but you didn't tell us they'd be here. How come that isn't rude?"

"Don't worry too much about it. We're leaving," says Uncle Dean.

"Oh, but I thought we could—" Laura starts. She looks at Dad, then at Uncle Dean. Whatever she'd been going to say, she stops. Then she goes on: "Well, at least let us send you off with some bagels! And leftovers!"

She quickly pulls out a few Tupperwares from the fridge, packs them in a public radio tote bag along with some of the bagels and cream cheese, and hands the bag to Alonso with a big smile.

"¡Muchísimas gracias!" Alonso says, and it's not that he's exaggerating his accent or anything, but there's something about the way he says it that makes me think he's speaking Spanish *at* them? Then Dad and Laura have to hug Grandma, and then me, and then, finally, we get to leave.

TWENTY-ONE

YOU'D THINK THAT WITH ALL THE THANKSGIVING drama, big things would have changed right away, but they didn't. What did happen is that Uncle Dean started coming over more. Just generally being around, mostly without Alonso. He brought over takeout from Vince's 24 Hours. He fixed the sliding closet door that's been off its track ever since I can remember. Grandma and I would just leave it open so we wouldn't have to mess with it. It was funny to see the door actually closed, and it made me wonder if the coats and hats were scared to be in the dark.

I slide it open again. It's a cedar closet, so it smells amazing. When I was little, I liked hiding in it, which, come to think of it, might have been how the door got off track in the first place, from Grandma yanking it open to find me.

I FEEL A LITTLE AWKWARD WHEN I COME into Youth Council, but not for long, because right away, Yesenia waves me over to sit next to her. Then she claps to get everyone's attention. "Okay! So what we're gonna do today is weed for condition. Like weeding a garden, except we're looking for books that are falling apart and messed up. Then we bring them back here so Alonso can do the next part. Right?" She looks at Alonso, who gives her a double thumbs-up.

Enrique asks, "What's the next part?"

Faisal asks, "Can we keep them if they're too messed up to be in the library?"

Linh asks, "Can we do, like, a craft with the messed-up books? I want to make something."

Alonso clears his throat. "In order: Enrique, the next part is to withdraw them from the collection in the computer so nobody tries to check them out. Faisal, it depends—some, possibly, yes. Others we might need to save for the Friends of the Library sale, and Linh, if you know any crafts that use books or book pages and you want to teach us, that's great. We won't have time today, but that sounds good for next week. Also, thank you, Yesenia, for introducing the activity; let me add that we'll be working just in the teen section, okay?"

"Do they think we can't tell if an adult book is messed up? Or, like, board books?" I ask. "We know what happens to board books—they literally get chewed up by drooly babies."

I don't actually care that much, but it doesn't seem fair that we wouldn't be allowed in the other sections, and also everyone else was asking things, so I wanted to ask something, too.

"Alex, it's not that people don't trust you all; it's just there are other volunteers lined up for other sections, and we don't want to make it so they don't have anything to do, okay? You all ready to get out there?"

It takes a few more minutes of wrangling about where exactly to put ourselves. We land on everyone starting out in the part of the stacks that corresponds to the first letter of our last name. And we clarify whether it's just book books or graphic novels, also. "Definitely do the graphic novels," Alonso says. "They get read to death real fast."

"Read . . . to . . . DEATH," says Enrique in a horror-movie-trailer voice. Then we disperse to our various parts of the teen section.

I get hung up on figuring out how messed up qualifies as messed up enough to be weeded. If there are pages missing or if someone spilled something and the pages have gone wavy, clearly that's bad enough, but what if there's just, like, a little tear on the cover? (If we were weeding to get rid of cheesy covers, that would be easier, but also there wouldn't be many books left.)

I decide to only weed the most obviously messed-up ones and stack up a few next to me: One has a lot of pages torn out, one has gum stuck to the inside back cover (gross), and on the third, someone drew devil horns and a beard on the person on the cover and also stabbed their eyes out with a pencil (creepy). Then I read the back cover of that one; it sounds possibly interesting. I open it to see if the first page is decent. I haven't been reading much lately except for school and stuff online. It's been a while since I've fallen into a story.

This one I like, because even though I don't have any idea what's going to happen (or why someone wanted to make the person on the cover an eyeless devil), I just like the way the character sees things. Like, how they describe the world is different, but in a way that lets me in so I can see it that way, too.

Someone taps my shoulder and I jump.

"Hey, reading on the job?" says Uncle Dean.

"Hi," I say, ignoring the question, because it wasn't a question as much as a very weak joke.

"You planning on staying late to study tonight?"

I forgot to check in with him. We're still doing that.

"No," I say. "Just going home after. Are you coming over?"

I feel a little itchy just talking to him out in the open like this. Enrique hasn't asked again about me being in trouble. Maybe he forgot about it or something, but I hate the idea of people seeing me talking to Uncle Dean and thinking—I don't know. Bad things.

"Hadn't planned on it tonight—we'll see. How's she been? Taking her pills?"

That's the one thing Uncle Dean and I have organized between us. The only thing, other than how I'm supposed to check in with him when I come to the library after school. We keep track of how many pills she has to take at different times, and Uncle Dean has even started helping with sorting them into the pill organizer that has the days of the week on it. I was amazed that she let him.

"Yeah," I say. "She's getting low on the cholesterol one, but I think she was going to the pharmacy for a refill today."

"Oof, that's something else we're gonna have to talk about," he says. "Driving. Not looking forward to that conversation."

When he says "we," I don't know if he means just him and Grandma, or him and Grandma and me. And I'm kind of glad he's telling me that he's worrying about the driving conversation, but also I'm kind of uncomfortable because I don't know if I'm supposed to help with it, or what helping would even be—like, would we be telling her we don't think she should drive at all? Or not drive alone? Or what?

And then I worry because I haven't been worrying about her driving, but now it seems like I should have been?

It's still so long before I can start learning to drive. I wish I were older.

Enrique comes by with a huge stack of beat-up Narutos that he's cradling in both arms, keeping it braced with his chin. Just as he's walking past us, one of the paperbacks slides out of the stack, and then he drops them all.

"I'll help you pick them up," I say, and I'm blushing for no reason, except when I think about it, I realize the reason is that I don't like how Enrique has seen me talking to my uncle, who he doesn't know is my uncle, and why do I even care anyway? I don't know. I grab a bunch of the fallen, battered Narutos, along with the few messed-up novels I found, and take them back to the meeting room.

Linh's there, too, and gets excited to see all the Narutos. "I'm going to cut out characters from a bunch of different ones and do a collage to make a totally new story!"

"No you're not, I'm gonna take them home and read them!" says Enrique.

"There was nothing good in my section—it's not fair!" says Linh.

Faisal comes in with a few books, then Yesenia, walking slow because she's balancing books on top of her head. "My balance is undefeated!" she says, and the books slide off her head onto the carpet.

"HEY! Can you all please just—get it together?"

Alonso has never sounded this mad. I bend down to pick up Yesenia's fallen books—she does, too—and once we've got them picked up, we don't know what to do, so we just stand awkwardly holding them. Linh and Enrique are still glaring at each other, and Faisal just looks confused.

"Come on, you heard him," I say. "Let's just leave everything here for now, and we can figure out who's doing what with the books next week."

And for some reason, everyone actually listens to me. We stack the books on the table by Alonso, so he can scan their barcodes and take them out of the system, and then people start leaving. I pretend to need to tie my shoe, which is very dumb because they are both clearly tied, so I pretend that I need to tie one more tightly, and that's when Yesenia, who was waiting for me, I think, leaves, too, with an exaggerated sigh that I can't tell if she means for me, Alonso, or both of us, and she kind of skips out instead of walking, but somehow it's an angry skip? I'll have to text her later, but right now I need to talk to Alonso.

"Are you okay?" I ask.

Alonso has been making his way through the messy stack of

battered books. He scans another of the Narutos Enrique and Linh were fighting over, sets it down. "Aren't I supposed to be the one asking you that, Alex?"

"Things are happening to you, too, though," I say.

"They are. Thanks for noticing. Not your job to fix, but thanks."

What is my job, though? That's what I still can't seem to figure out.

"HEY!" YESENIA POPS HER HEAD OUT FROM the stacks when I leave the meeting room. She was actually waiting for me after all. "Hey, you know what we all totally forgot about?"

"Hi! And no, I mean, if we all forgot, then I don't know?"

Saying the word *forgot* gives me a different feeling now, but I push that feeling down.

"The city-council-budget-vote thing, I think it's really soon; my mom said like next Monday, I think?"

"Oof, that's less than a week." I look around. There are people at all the tables and computers, so there isn't any place for us to sit, which is pretty much usual for this time of day.

"Yeah," Yesenia says. "But people don't always make up their minds until the very last minute, so maybe we can still do something?"

"What were you thinking we could do?" We keep walking around the stacks as we talk, stopping every so often to look at titles. I pull a fat science fiction novel off the shelf because I like how the type on the spine looks, read the back cover and see it's the fifth in a series, put it back.

She sighs. "I don't know. Something with social media?"

"Do city council people pay attention to social media?"

"Dunno."

We've wandered over to the newspapers section, which is a bad idea, because the men who read them—it's basically all men for some reason—they like to stay all day, and they don't like anyone else being there. One of them glares at us, so we head over to the DVDs.

I'm glad we're talking about this. It's serious, it's important, and also it's not quite as personal as directly discussing family. I think of the field hockey drills day in gym with her, and how easy and nice it was, and promise myself that I won't take her friendship for granted.

Yesenia tugs on my sleeve. "What if we did like an art thing? Like a big poster or something showing all the ways people use the library? And we could, I don't know, drop it off at city hall before they vote on the budget?"

"That's a seriously good idea," I say. "Remember when we did that field trip and met the mayor?"

It was back in third grade, after our class finished the bland propaganda project that made Rachel mad and made me and PJ best friends.

"Yeah, remember how he kept going on about us being the future of Failin? And it's like, um, excuse me, we're actually the right *now* of Failin? Just because we can't vote or give them money doesn't mean we don't, like, exist. But yeah, I was thinking everybody could do different pieces."

We decide to start our pieces tonight and tell other Youth Council people to make their own, and then we'll combine them all over the weekend.

Yesenia gets permission from her mom to come over, because I remember I have poster board left over from last year's science fair and also a bunch of markers and colored pencils.

Grandma's not home when we get to the house, and I feel myself seize up right away. It's not book club night, and I don't know where she is. But I can't stay rigid, because Yesenia's with me, and she's petting Snufkin and asking if he missed her, and he's purring really loud. I manage to get out all the art stuff for us and also some snickerdoodles that are kind of stale but homemade. We sit at the breakfast bar to get to work.

"Your house is so quiet! It's crazy!" says Yesenia. "If we were at my house, there could be ten Snufkins all purring at the top of their lungs and you still wouldn't be able to hear them."

I like Yesenia's vision of multiple Snufkins, but another one comes to my mind: "What if it was just one, but, like, really big? Like a six-foot-tall Snufkin."

"Ha! Then my brothers would just want to climb on him and ride him." She takes a snickerdoodle. "Ooh these are good!" I'm glad she likes them.

She starts drawing a giant Snufkin, but then we can't figure out how to connect that to the library, so we turn over the poster board and start again. She draws Tía Gabi holding a stack of romance novels—you can tell they're romance novels because she puts hearts on the spines—and she's standing next to a printer that's spitting out pages. It's a little hard to tell the printer is a printer, so Yesenia labels it.

I worry that some people might think romance novels aren't important, so I try to think of library things that feel like no one could say they were too frivolous or fun to be worth paying for with tax dollars. I draw Alonso sitting at the Tax Help table looking helpful. Then I do a sign that says RÉSUMÉ WORKSHOP, with the lady whose name I don't know who wears the cool print dresses standing next to it smiling.

Neither of them really look like themselves. I mean, you can sort of tell it's Alonso from the ponytail, but I gave up on trying to draw a cool print after messing up three squids, so I made the dress a solid purple instead and just gave her big earrings that are supposed to be squids but look like maybe they're ghosts, or umbrellas.

There's still a lot of room on the poster when we're done, but that means there'll be space for other people's drawings, too. Yesenia says she can tell her mom to tell Enrique's mom to tell him to draw something.

"I can see if PJ can send something we could print out and paste on," I say.

"Yeah! FaceTime her! Then I can say hi!"

"My phone isn't great with video," I lie. "And I think she has practice right now anyway?" I don't actually know this, but it's always likely. And I don't know if PJ is still mad at Yesenia for spreading gossip, or if she'd be mad that I'm hanging out with her.

Or maybe I just don't want to share PJ, which is weird because we were all friends before PJ moved, but still.

"Well, take pictures of what we have so far and send them to her!"

So I do that, or at least I take the pictures, including some of me and Yesenia pointing at different parts of what we drew. Maybe I won't send those to PJ.

"Does she like Portland? How's she doing, even?" Yesenia asks, taking another snickerdoodle.

"There are things about it she likes, yeah. The swimming stuff is better, I guess."

Yesenia nods. "That's good—she's been all about that forever. And is it, like, easier for her moms? Are people less, you know, messed up about gay people there?"

I think about the family dinner PJ told me about. Having a bunch of friends to have a holiday with does sound like it's probably easier and maybe more fun than mostly just having Kyla's family, who maybe don't even like Rachel that much.

But I say, "I don't know. I mean, I think there are homophobic people everywhere unfortunately."

"Yeah, true." Yesenia looks at her phone. "Oh yikes, I have to go! I think this is really good, though, what we have so far. Do you have, like, a tube or something I could roll it up in, or a plastic bag?"

I find a garbage bag, and we get the poster into it, along with the markers in case she wants to add stuff, and Yesenia heads home.

I stopped thinking about Grandma for a while when we were

drawing, but now it's been over an hour since I got home, and she's still not here. We were just at the grocery Sunday, and it's not book club night. She might be at the pharmacy? Sometimes it takes them a while to fill the prescriptions, and she likes to just stay there instead of having to take two trips, one to drop them off and another to pick them up. But she didn't leave a note, and she hasn't called me.

Obviously I should call her.

Find out where she is.

When she'll be home.

Then I see her phone.

On the counter, plugged in, charging, useless.

I'm rigid. Well, not totally rigid. I'm holding on to my elbows and kind of rocking back and forth, staring at the breakfast bar. Cookie crumbs and colored pencils. Snufkin hops up onto the breakfast bar. He'll want to eat the crumbs, because they have butter, but I shouldn't let him. I grab him. He hisses. I squeeze him too tight. He yowls; I drop him; I'm crying.

A knock at the door. Did Yesenia forget something? I wipe my eyes and sniff and go to open it, but it's already opening by the time I get there: It's Uncle Dean with a bag from Vince's 24 Hours again. I guess he has a key now. Or he still has a key?

"She has the car, and I don't know where she is," I say, and I'm crying again.

Uncle Dean puts the bag down on the little table by the door. "Have you tried calling her?"

"No," I say, my voice all shaky and strange, "because she didn't take her phone. It's here, on the counter."

He breathes in, then out, slow. The door's still open. It's cold outside and dark. I hope Yesenia got home okay.

He says, "Ah hell, kiddo."

I am so much more scared because I can tell he's scared, too.

"Probably just slipped her mind," he says, "probably just went on a quick errand—"

Then he just stops. Breathes slow again.

We haven't been, like, affectionate at all before, but I find myself stepping closer to him, and this is not how I imagined I would hug my uncle for the first time, but suddenly it's what's happening, and he hugs me back, and hugging doesn't solve anything, but it's a kind of comfort I didn't know I needed until I had it. We hang onto each other for a while. "Okay. Okay, okay," Uncle Dean says, like if he says it enough times, things actually will be. Then he pats my back awkwardly, and we both let go.

"Alex," he says then. "Hey. Alex. Hey. She's probably just fine. She'll probably be home soon. Okay?"

"Okay."

TWENTY-TWO

grandma got in a car accident

she hit a phone pole real hard and it pretty much broke, like, split

and she's hurt

the airbag inflated so it's not as bad as it could be

car is super messed up though

and she's definitely bruised and like shaken and sore

she didn't hurt anyone else which is really good

but we're at the emergency room

she's mad at us and says she's fine

she's not

I stare at the texts, delete them.

Because it's not like PJ can do anything, and I don't want her to think I only text when something bad happens.

Instead I type:

> do you want to draw something for the library?

> youth council is doing a big poster of all the ways people use FPL

> so city council will want to give them $

> it has to be soon though

> like by this weekend

> sure! i'll do it tonight

> did you like assign things or can i draw whatever

> draw whatever!

Seems like I should follow that exclamation point with an emoji, but I can't push my fake cheer any further. What's the difference between pretending things are okay and actually lying? Maybe there is no difference.

PJ sends a thumbs-up.

I shift my weight on the slippery plastic chair.

They put Grandma in a wheelchair. She keeps trying to get up, and Uncle Dean keeps telling her she just needs to sit tight and wait a little longer; he knows it's hard.

A guy with a beard and a knee brace and a U Pull U Save work shirt has been yelling into his phone about how he can't make his shift. "You think I'm lying?"

A nurse comes out from the doorway of the actual place where they examine people. "Kathy Eager?"

Uncle Dean and I get up. I take the handles of Grandma's wheelchair. "Is it okay if I push you?"

"I suppose," she says.

"Put your feet on the footrest," says Uncle Dean. She does, and she winces.

"Hurts," she says.

"Well, that's why we're here," he says. I start pushing.

Meanwhile, the bearded guy has limped over to the nurse. "Tell my boss I'm at the emergency room."

"Sir, I'm looking for Kathy Eager right now."

"Look!" He holds up his phone to film the nurse. "This proves it. See?"

"We're coming," says Uncle Dean, waving at the nurse.

But the nurse won't let me go back with her, only Uncle Dean. I could get mad and I kind of am, but I'm also a little bit relieved, and besides that, ashamed of being relieved. "Write down what they tell you," I say. "I need to know all of it."

I didn't bring anything but my phone, since we were obviously in a giant rush when we found out what had happened, and in theory I could do homework on my phone, but in reality I can't. I suddenly think of the bag Uncle Dean brought from Vince's 24 Hours, still on the little table by the door. Snufkin has probably gotten into it by now. I hope he hasn't made himself sick.

Because I have my phone, I decide it's okay to wander. After walking around for a while, I find the gift shop. It's closed. The best thing I can see through the window is a very large stuffed giraffe with a stethoscope and glasses. "Dr. Giraffe," I whisper. "What's the prognosis, Dr. Giraffe?"

I take a picture of Dr. Giraffe and send it to PJ captioned *meet doctor giraffe* without really thinking about it.

> where is that?

> hospital gift shop

The phone starts ringing. I drop it, then scramble to pick it up. "Hey," PJ says, "hospital?"

"Hi. Yeah. Grandma had a car accident." My voice is wobbly, but because PJ called—actually called, so I know she really wants to know—I'm able to keep talking. "Uncle Dean's with her. They're looking at her now, but I'm not allowed to be back with them so I'm just, like, roaming around the hospital. Which is how I found Dr. Giraffe."

I sit cross-legged on a bench outside the gift shop, sideways so I can still see the window display.

"Oh my god, Alex, that's super scary. I'm so sorry! Were you in the car, too?"

"No. And she didn't hit anyone, but the car is really messed up."

"Oof," PJ says. "I wish I could hug you right now."

"I wish you could, too. Thanks for calling me."

"What was I going to do, NOT call after you said *hospital*? I mean come on."

"I know. It's really good to hear your voice."

Then I don't know what to say. I look at Dr. Giraffe again. "I just realized they can't just be Dr. Giraffe, because that's like calling someone Dr. Human. What should their name be?"

"Artemisia Gloss-Goldfarb," PJ says immediately.

"Paging Dr. Gloss-Goldfarb," I say. "That's perfect."

The phone vibrates with a text.

> Where are you? They're going to keep her overnight for observation.

"I have to go," I say. "Thank you, again."

"I love you," says PJ.

"I love you, too," I say, and end the call, happiness foaming up, just for a minute, over worry and fear.

"That's the first time we've said it to each other, Dr. Gloss-Goldfarb," I whisper.

TWENTY-THREE

"SO, YOU SHOULD STAY AT OUR PLACE TONIGHT," Uncle Dean told me when we got in the car. "Stop by the house and pick up some things first, of course."

"I can't just leave Snufkin alone." Part of me wants to see what Uncle Dean and Alonso's place looks like, but a bigger part wants to sleep in my own bed, and maybe before that to see what else I can find about my mom—and Uncle Dean, for that matter—in Grandma's room.

Then I feel like a horrible person for even thinking up that scheme, when I should be worrying about Grandma with one hundred percent of my brain. Well, one hundred percent minus the part that's happy PJ told me she loves me. Which is like another hundred percent. Maybe percentages don't work for this.

"He'll be fine. He's a cat," says Uncle Dean.

"You're just saying that. You don't know!"

Then we don't say anything for a while.

Grandma has broken ribs and maybe other things wrong. They're waiting on imaging results, Uncle Dean told me. I don't really know what that means, but I don't think he does, either, so I'm not going to ask.

When we get home—my home, I mean, although I guess it used to be Uncle Dean's home, too, and maybe it still is, in a way—Snufkin is fine. He clawed up the plastic bag but didn't get to the actual food in it.

"I'll be fine staying here by myself," I say, petting Snufkin.

"Not gonna happen. Come on, get your stuff together."

"Shouldn't we bring stuff to the hospital for Grandma, too? She'll feel better if she's in her own nightgown."

"She'll be asleep by now. I'll go back first thing tomorrow."

"I need to go, too!"

"She wouldn't want you missing school. I'll see how she is, see what they want to do. Right now, just please get what you need for overnight and tomorrow, okay? I'll feed this guy and scoop the litter box."

In my room I have a hard time figuring out what to bring. An outfit for tomorrow is easy, but it's weird to think Uncle Dean and Alonso will be seeing me in pajamas. I mean, I wear sweats anyway, not anything, like, small and frilly, but still.

My brain flashes to Grandma in the hospital, without her own nightgown. Probably they have her in some flimsy thing. What if she's cold?

How many times can I cry today?

My phone vibrates. PJ's sent a drawing of Alonso reading to a bunch of tiny kids, underneath a big STORY TIME sign. (Her version of Alonso looks more like him than mine does.) That's so smart. Everybody likes little kids being read to.

> i know you're probably not thinking about the library rn

> but i just did this instead of homework so

> it's really good

> thanks

> my moms' idea

> "tug the heartstrings" they said

> they are tugged

> yanked on, even

> wait that sounds bad

> you know what i mean though

"Get a move on!" Uncle Dean calls. I don't know what he's in a hurry for. Maybe it's weird for him to be in this house. Maybe he just wants to get home to Alonso.

"Get a move on" is something Grandma says, too.

I get a move on.

ALONSO AND UNCLE DEAN'S APARTMENT IS

really small. You walk into a kind of kitchen/dining room/living room all at once. There's a little round table with two chairs, refrigerator, sink, cabinets, and then on the opposite side of the same room, a futon couch, some bookshelves, and a TV. Right past the kitchendininglivingroom there's a narrow hallway to a couple of other rooms, probably a bathroom and, I guess, their bedroom. At the end of the hall there's another bookshelf, tall and skinny.

"Hi, Alex, welcome. And I'm sorry."

I expect Alonso to look different somehow in his own space, but he doesn't, not really. Just that his hair is down, out of its ponytail. And he's not wearing his library badge around his neck. I see it, though, hanging on a key rack by the door. Elephants' heads, their trunks are the hooks.

"Your place is nice," I say. It is, even though it's small. Everything's the right size.

"Thank you. Come on in. There's soup."

"Dumplings, too," says Uncle Dean from behind me.

"Great!" says Alonso.

It's late to be eating dinner, but we're all hungry. Alonso's soup has chicken and peppers and carrots and tomatoes and rice, and he microwaves the dumplings so they're hot again, and they offer me one of the chairs, but I say I'd rather sit on the floor, so Alonso puts mine on a cute tray with robots on it, and I balance it carefully on my lap and lean against the futon while I eat.

I stare at the shelves that surround the TV: comics, science fiction, some photography collections. I realize I'm looking for anything gay. Then I realize it might not actually be obvious which of the books are gay. Then I think what a funny way of putting it that is, like the books themselves are gay. Like they're only attracted to books of the same gender. What gender would that be?

"How'd she take it all?" Alonso asks, and I think, *I'm right here*. But he means Grandma.

Uncle Dean dabs at his mouth with his napkin. "Mad at first, but once, I guess, the adrenaline wore off and she could tell how banged up she is, well, she quieted down."

"What happened with the car?"

"Got it towed to Gail's for now. Probably totaled."

"So, one good thing comes out of this—no car, you don't have to tell her she has to stop driving."

"Huh, you may have a point."

"Why you keep me around."

They both smile, and there's something so good about those smiles, like, I can tell how tired they are but also how glad they are to be home with each other. It makes me feel like I'm eavesdropping, so I stay silent, eating my dumplings and soup super slowly and carefully so I don't spill.

When I'm done, I take the robot tray over to the sink and turn to Uncle Dean and Alonso. It looks like they're done, too, so I go to take their plates. Alonso gets up. "No no no, Alex, you're our guest. There's no need."

"I don't mind."

"Yes, but I do. You've had a hard day. You don't have to do anything."

"Okay, thanks." But if I'm not going to wash the dishes, that means I don't have anything to do. I wash my hands since I'm already by the sink, and wipe them on my pants. "Is it okay if I take something to read?"

"What do you think?" Alonso grins in a did-you-forget-I'm-a-librarian way.

"I mean I figured you wouldn't mind, but sometimes people have stuff they don't want other people messing with."

"Grab anything you want," says Alonso. "Nothing's off limits."

"Other than the beers," says Uncle Dean, opening the refrigerator to take one.

I stare at the bookcase again while Uncle Dean sips his beer and Alonso does the dishes. I wonder what they'd be doing if it were a normal evening. Watching a show? Making out? I blush.

I find a book I've already read and pull it off the shelf.

"Hey," says Uncle Dean, "have you got homework you should be doing?"

"Alonso already said I don't have to do anything."

"That was about chores. What about it? Essay to write? A problem set?"

A set of problems. Sounds about right.

"I don't remember," I say, which is kind of a lie, because the assignments are all online. "I don't think I should go to school tomorrow anyway. I need to be there for Grandma."

"I know you want to be, kiddo," Uncle Dean says. "I just don't know—"

I interrupt. My heartbeat is speedy, and my cheeks are hot. "Even if she thinks I'm my mom, it'll help her if I'm there. She's used to me. She doesn't really know— I mean, she's just getting to know you. Know you again, I mean. Know who you are now. You know?" I sound ridiculous to myself. All those *knows*.

"Well," Uncle Dean says slowly, "you might have a point."

"What did you fight about, back then?"

I didn't know I wanted to talk about this, but suddenly it's the only thing in my head.

Uncle Dean takes another sip of his beer, not looking at me.

"A lot of things, Alex. We were pretty far apart about a lot of things. And I was taking some wrong turns, back then."

Far apart and *wrong turns* make it sound like he and Grandma were, like, physically far away from each other, and I guess they kind of were, but they were also, I think, mostly in the same town and sometimes, if he started at FPL before she retired, even in the same building.

Alonso's dishcloth makes a squeaky sound against the plate he's drying. I'd almost forgotten he was in the room. I guess I don't mind. Not that I could ask him to leave if I did. It's his apartment. Their apartment. Not mine.

"Will you tell me what the things were?" I ask.

Uncle Dean sighs. "I don't know, Alex. Maybe someday."

"Did Grandma take wrong turns, too?"

This is as close as I can make myself get to asking if she kicked him out or disowned him or was homophobic in some other extreme and dramatic way, which I know used to happen a lot and is obviously also still happening.

Uncle Dean rubs the back of his neck and looks at the elephant-head key rack, like the elephants might know the answer. They never forget, after all.

"We talked past each other. A lot. Sometimes just didn't talk."

I don't like admitting when I don't understand something, but this seems important. "What does talking past each other mean?"

"What it sounds like. Words are being spoken but not really heard. By either party."

"Oh." I think about how many times I've thought I was having conversations but it was that instead. Like when you're not really listening, just waiting for the other person to stop talking so you can say your thing. It also makes me think of aiming—like, are you trying to make your words go somewhere that isn't actually to the other person? Like when there's someone else you want to impress, who's close enough to hear. Or when you just want to hear your own voice, to make yourself feel better about yourself.

Alonso clears his throat. "Let's make it an early night, but first we'll fold out the couch for you and get it all set up with sheets and blankets."

"You don't have to," I say. "I mean, sheets and blankets are good, but I'm fine sleeping on it just how it is."

Unfolded, it would take up too much space in the room. So would I.

TWENTY-FOUR

I DIDN'T END UP GOING TO SCHOOL. UNCLE Dean called and talked to the office, and that was a whole thing: He had to prove to them who he was, and at one point he was yelling, and I tried to pretend like I wasn't in the room. But at the same time I was glad he was sticking up for me being able to see Grandma, even though I was also worried about seeing her.

Grandma was . . . subdued, I think, would be the right word. She really didn't have much to say except that she needed to get home, which she said a bunch of times. They sent her home with a wheelchair to use, which I don't really understand, since I thought it was just her ribs that were messed up and I don't know why a wheelchair would help with that, but I guess there are other things wrong, too. They also gave her a sort of booster to put on the toilet seat to make it easier to sit down on and get up from. The occupational therapist wants Uncle Dean to measure stuff like how tall her bed is in case she needs something to help her get in and out of it, too. I said I'd help with the measuring.

I told Uncle Dean to write everything down that the medical

people said about Grandma, but I don't think he did. And I don't know if I actually want to hear it, even though I feel like I should.

Maybe I would if it was Dr. Gloss-Goldfarb telling me. I wonder what her voice would sound like? I kind of wish the gift shop had been open so I'd have been able to buy her and take her home. Then I feel dumb and babyish for wishing that, but also I feel like holding a stuffed giraffe doctor might be comforting, except I wouldn't want anyone to see me doing it. Except maybe PJ.

Anyway, when we get home, I think Grandma will want to go to sleep, but what she actually does is look through the mail, mostly ads, and then she needs her checkbook to pay the water bill, because, unlike 99 percent of everyone, she doesn't do online payment. "Got to get this handled," she says, and makes out the check. Is her handwriting shakier, harder to read?

My phone vibrates. It's from Yesenia: a photo of all our library drawings, even PJ's—I remembered to forward it to her—and I guess Yesenia must have printed it out and pasted everything together. It honestly looks pretty janky, but also sincere.

I text Yesenia back:

> cool!

I show Grandma the photo.

"Nice job," she says. "Good for you!"

Meanwhile Uncle Dean has been on the phone—with Alonso, I'm pretty sure, but he's talking too quietly for me to hear.

Grandma puts the water bill check in the envelope, seals it, then puts on a stamp, kind of crooked.

"There, that's handled," she says. "Put it in the mailbox for me, will you, Joanie?"

I put it in the mailbox.

> we're home from the hospital
>
> i should be doing homework but i can't brain

of course you can't!

PJ sends me a video of some capybaras in a hot springs with flowers all around them. Some of them are eating the flowers. They look very calm.

> i wish i was a calm capybara
>
> that we both were actually

that could be another verse for mole in the ground

except it's hard to rhyme capybara

unless you put the emphasis on different syllables in the third line . . .

if i was a calm caPYbarA,

i could wear a ti-ar-a

wish i was a calm capybara

> yeah exactly, that's perfect

Uncle Dean has finished his phone call, and now he's started to do all the measuring the occupational therapist asked for. If I'm not doing homework, which obviously I'm not, I should help him. But I can't make myself move from where I am, which is sitting at the table where Grandma is, too. And measuring is really a one-person job, isn't it?

"Can I get you anything? Do you need to lie down?" I ask, to feel like I'm doing something.

"Oh, I'm all right, Alex. Don't worry. Your grandma's a tough old bird."

What switch is it in her head that flips to sometimes know me and sometimes turn me into my mom? I guess no one knows. Because if they did, they could just do surgery, or give her a pill or something, to make sure it flips to the right answer.

There's a knock at the door. "I'll get it!" Now I can move. I shoot out of my chair like the knock is the starting gun for the Race to Make Sure Grandma Doesn't Move More than She's Supposed to and Hurt Herself More than She Already Has.

It's Alonso. He's got a duffel bag. "For your uncle." He hands it to me. "I can't stay; I'm just on lunch."

For a second I think, *Did they just break up?* My face must have done something, because Alonso says, "He's going to have to stay with you all for a while, as I understand it. To help out your grandma?"

"Oh. Right. Okay." I knew this. That's why Uncle Dean is here now instead of at work. "Friday's her book club. She's going to want to go," I say. "And her friends from there, they should know, and I think some of them are from the library? I don't know their phone numbers."

"Maybe see if they can meet at your house this time? Sorry, Alex, you'll have to talk to your uncle. I need to get going."

"Sorry, of course, thanks," I say, closing the door.

Grandma has fallen asleep in her wheelchair. I walk by her as quietly as I can and back to her bedroom, where Uncle Dean is standing next to the bed holding the tape measure.

"Alonso brought this for you. Grandma fell asleep? Is it okay for her to sleep in the chair?"

Uncle Dean wipes his eyes. Then he takes the duffel bag. "For a while, sure, I guess. Unless, unless her head gets to be at a bad angle."

"Where are you going to sleep? I mean, tonight and stuff?"

Uncle Dean smiles. It's not a good smile, like the one he smiled at Alonso last night one million years ago. It's more a grimace, like when you trip and fall and someone asks if you're okay and you're not, but you don't want to say. "In my very own childhood bedroom. Or, as you may know it, the spare room. She never did get rid of the bed, so, yeah."

Something else to add to the way-too-long list of things I haven't ever thought about but clearly should have.

We go to the spare room. His old room. There's nothing in it that's, like, decor. Just a bed and a dresser and a floor lamp that always lists to one side. I wonder what it looked like when he lived here.

He puts the duffel on the bed; it raises a little dust. No one has ever actually stayed in the spare room as long as I can remember. When PJ came for sleepovers, she'd bring a sleeping bag and sleep on the floor in my room.

Have I always been sleeping in my mom's bed? I don't know a lot about furniture, but I know beds are expensive, so, probably. I can't decide if this is good—like I've been somehow closer to my mom all this time—or creepy.

"So, my room was my mom's?" I ask.

"Sure was! She never told you?" Uncle Dean opens the top drawer of the dresser, which sticks a little and squeaks. It's empty, which I knew, because I do come in here from time to time, but it's still somehow disappointing? Like Uncle Dean opening it should have been like Arthur pulling the sword out of the stone.

"We don't talk about the past like that," I say. Another part of the upside-down mountain. "We should check on her."

I turn around and walk back to where Grandma is still asleep, snoring a little now. Her head seems like it's at an okay angle, but it's hard to know.

"Let's not disturb her," says Uncle Dean quietly, from behind me.

"Okay. Can I talk to you, though? In the kitchen?"

From the kitchen we can still see her and get to her fast if we need to.

Here's what I know about Grandma's book club: It's all women. They mostly talk about picture books. There are teachers in it, and I think a library person or two, but not Alonso. It's been going on for years. They mostly meet at the same person's house, someone who really likes baking and, I guess, having people over. Grandma took me with her once, and they all thought my Actual Kid Perspective on the picture books was super fascinating, which was nice, but also stressful, because it felt like I was suddenly in school and I hadn't, like, prepared my opinions or anything.

I explain to Uncle Dean about how book club works, how I

think Grandma would like seeing her friends, how Alonso said maybe they could come here.

"I don't know, Alex—seems like a lot of trouble to go to, and she might not even be comfortable with it."

"I can make cookies," I say. "And I'll look on her computer to find the group email."

Grandma's snoring turns into a snort. She opens her eyes. "Hi, Grandma!" I say, too loud, hoping that by calling her Grandma right away I can make the switch in her head stay on the right setting, here with us now. "We were talking about book club Friday. I was thinking they could come here?"

"Ugh, need to get my teeth brushed," says Grandma. "They have that furry feeling. How do I get the brakes off this thing again?"

"Let me help," I say, but Uncle Dean is there before I am, showing Grandma the levers that unlock the wheels.

"You need the restroom while you're at it?" he asks.

"No no, I'm fine." She pushes off toward the bathroom.

"You sure?"

"I said *fine*!"

He follows her anyway. Their voices get louder. He wants her to use the bathroom. She says she doesn't need it. He says to just try, see how the booster seat works.

"NO!"

If Uncle Dean were at the library right now, maybe someone would be waving a wine-juice-box around and calling him names. I wonder if that would be harder or easier.

Then I get on Grandma's computer and look for the book club email.

TWENTY-FIVE

NOBODY BUT ME THOUGHT IT WAS A GOOD idea for book club to happen at our house, it turned out. The usual host said it was too close to the meeting to change the location, and Grandma said she didn't have the energy.

What happens instead is that book club women start to show up with food. Meatloaf. Lentil stew. Lasagna. One brought a Grumpy Grandpa's take-n-bake pizza and said she couldn't cook but wanted to help out anyway. Like Alonso when he dropped off the duffel bag, they all say they can't stay, and I don't know if it's because they actually can't stay, or if they don't want to tire Grandma out with too much chitchat (that's what one of them said), or if seeing Grandma makes them uncomfortable.

It's Sunday afternoon now. I'm in the living room trying to do homework, Grandma's napping—she's been doing a lot of that, which is good, I guess—and another book club woman, who's brought a cake, is talking to Uncle Dean in the front doorway.

She hasn't actually handed him the cake. So far she's talked about what a shock it was to hear about the accident, and what a blessing it is that no one else was hurt, and also what a blessing it is that Uncle Dean is staying with Grandma. "You know, most times in situations like this, that'd fall to a daughter," she says.

Uncle Dean just looks at her.

"Now, I know this isn't the place or the time," says Cake Woman, "but I have to tell you, I've been keeping an eye on her for a while, and I'm not sure how much longer coming to our group will really be, well, viable for her?"

Cake Woman hands Uncle Dean the cake, finally. "You know," she goes on, "as it gets harder for her to follow conversations and such."

"You're right—it isn't the place or the time," Uncle Dean says, and shuts the door in her face.

Then he looks at me like he's just remembered I was in the room. "Should have thanked her for the cake, I guess."

"No you shouldn't have. She was awful, and I bet her stupid cake is bad. We shouldn't eat it. Can we, like, destroy it?"

Uncle Dean barks out a laugh. "Wow, kid, you're your mom's daughter, all right! Let's."

I take the cake into the backyard and put it on the ground. It's been cold and rainy, so the ground is muddy, which is a good start already. Then I find us each a big stick. We clack our sticks together over the cake three times—we don't discuss doing that before we do it, we just both recognize it as the obviously right thing to do—and then take turns hitting it as though it's a very soft and motionless piñata.

The cake turns out to have some kind of gloppy cherry or raspberry or strawberry filling that I'm entirely certain would have been sickly sweet if we'd actually eaten it. So of course it looks increasingly like blood and guts, and it's more satisfying than I even would've thought it'd be, and we're cracking up the whole time as we smash and smear the stupid cake into oblivion.

AFTER I FINISHED MY HOMEWORK, WHICH was weirdly less hard than I thought it would be—maybe because it was all solving problems that had clear correct answers?—I got suddenly overtaken with the need to move furniture in my room.

Which probably has something to do with knowing that my room used to be my mom's, but I can't explain what.

The bed is just like the one in Uncle Dean's room. I don't know why I've never noticed that before. I wonder if they started out as bunk beds, like PJ has. Was there a time when Uncle Dean and my mom shared a room? Who got the top bunk?

I push the bed from where it was, sticking out into the middle of the room, so that the long side is against the wall. There's more floor space but also a whole herd of dust bunnies—or actually dust kittens is probably a better name for them since they're made partially from Snufkin's fur—a few random socks, and an old hair tie of PJ's that I immediately put in the jewelry box.

"What you up to?" Grandma asks from just outside the door. She's gotten really good with the wheelchair in the few days she's been home.

"Just moving some things around."

"Good for you!" Grandma's all-purpose encouragement. I love hearing it, and it makes me sad at the same time. "Yeah," I say, "but now I have to vacuum, though."

I come out of my room to get the vacuum from the hall closet. It's heavy and annoying, but vacuuming is a chore I don't mind. You can tell the difference, especially since we have the kind where you can see the dirt getting sucked up into it.

The carpet looks okay-ish when I'm done. Ish, because vacuuming just gets rid of the dust kittens; it doesn't magically make the carpet not old and beige, except for the part with the blue stain from when I didn't put the cap back on a pen one time. At least the shade of blue is kind of nice.

TWENTY-SIX

> i thought all the bad things had happened already but they're still happening

> i saw

> my moms showed me online

> yeah

> so the library is actually going to close

> which means uncle dean and alonso both won't have jobs

> IT'S SO UNFAIR

> it makes me extra mad because it like confirms what my mom thinks about Failin

> which means she and mama will be fighting again about if we should even visit my grandparents for xmas

> YOU HAVE TO STILL VISIT

> I KNOW

We send screenfuls of hearts and crying emojis.

IT FEELS TERRIBLE TO WALK INTO YOUTH

Council knowing it's probably one of the last ones we'll have. We don't even pretend that we'll get anything done; we just sit around the blanket, which still smells like orange oil, and are sad.

"Thanks for coming, everyone," Alonso says. "I bet you have a lot of questions."

"Yeah, like why is city council stupid?" says Enrique.

"They have a tough job, Enrique. There are a lot of competing priorities," says Alonso in his Talking to Troubled Teens voice. I get why he's being so reasonable; he'd probably be, like, setting a bad example or something if he agreed that city council is stupid. But I wish he would anyway.

Faisal asks, "So when we were finding the messed-up books, was that just a big waste of time? Because now they're going to, what, just get rid of it all? Sell it to Amazon or something?"

Alonso pulls his ponytail tighter. "Faisal, quite honestly, I can't tell you exactly what will happen with the collection, because it hasn't been decided. But I can tell you that your work was not a waste of time. All the work you all have done—and you've been doing it for a while!—has been important and valued, and I'm really proud of each of you for the commitment you've made, the time you've put in. It matters. And it matters that you're thoughtful to each other, too. Most of the time. Right? So. Right now, what's happened isn't what any of us wanted. I probably shouldn't have said that, but the budget vote is over—anyway, it's not what we would have wanted, but it's what happened, and so now we need to kind of just take some time to come to terms with the new reality and figure out where we go from here."

"I hate the new reality," says Linh.

"I do, too," says Yesenia. "But I made brownies? Because of, you know, everything." She gets a covered dish out of her backpack, takes the cover off, and passes the dish to Alonso.

"Technically," he says, "we're not supposed to have homemade food—"

"Come ON!" says Enrique.

Alonso keeps going: "Let me finish. I said technically we're not supposed to, but here in the new reality, I'm gonna let it slide." He picks up a brownie, takes a big bite. "Delicious," he says, and when they make their way to me and I take one, too, I strongly agree.

After Youth Council, Yesenia and I stay at the library and just kind of overall catch up. She's had her own family stuff going on, and we talk about it for a long time, or actually she talks and I listen, which is good both because I want to know about it, and because it reminds me that even though I've been feeling like everything in the world is happening to me personally, actually everything is happening to everyone. Just sometimes it seems like it happens to you more for a while—good more or bad more, depending—and then it sort of settles down. Like weather, maybe. Although weather affects you differently if you have a big fancy house like Dad and Laura than if you live in the ravine in a tent, so maybe it's not the best comparison. Or maybe that exact thing means it is.

TWENTY-SEVEN

HOW I THOUGHT I'D BE SPENDING MY SATURDAY: mostly doing homework and texting with PJ, helping Grandma.

How I'm actually spending it: Uncle Dean still doesn't think I can help Grandma by myself, which he is in fact right about, and so instead I'm with Alonso helping him pack up their apartment, because they're going to move in with me and Grandma for real.

I'm not the only one helping. Their friend Gail and their other friends Scott and Terry are here, too. Gail is the mechanic. I remembered her name as the one they towed Grandma's car to after the accident. It was actually totaled, which is a weird term. I wonder if originally it was a phrase, like, *totally destroyed*, but people started to shorten it? Or if it has to do with adding up all the damage, and if the total is more than the car is worth, then it's totaled? I know this is not an actually important thing to understand, but sometimes my brain gets hung up on small questions.

Because the apartment isn't very big (and, I guess, because some things are more private), Alonso has us assigned, kind of, to different rooms. He's in the bedroom by himself, Terry has the bathroom, Scott the hallway with the bookshelf, and me and

Gail are in the kitchendininglivingroom, wrapping up dishes and glasses. There's music on that I don't recognize but I like—it's energetic but not annoying.

"Aw, you still have the robot tray!" Gail says. "I found it at the antique mall and I had to get it," she tells me, holding it up, "because the robots look like them. See?"

I can't actually tell why Gail thinks that—maybe because the windup key at the back of one robot's neck kind of resembles Alonso's ponytail? But I nod and pretend I can, because I like that she told me, and I like that she got it at Faithful Angus, and I also like that she and the rest of them aren't making a big weird deal out of me being a kid. They're just treating me like a person.

Gail wraps the robot tray in newspaper and puts it in a box. Then she slides open the door to the apartment's tiny balcony, where there are a few pots with plants in them that look like they're probably dead. It is December, after all. "I'm gonna miss visiting you guys here," she says.

"So you're going to abandon us once we've moved?" Alonso calls from the bedroom. "I knew it!"

"I meant what I said. I'll miss visiting you *here*. I've always liked this place."

"Well, maybe you should take it, then. They do month-to-month. They'll raise the rent after we're out, of course, but you're flush, right?"

"Dave might object," says Gail. "He's pretty fond of our current situation."

I totally thought Gail was gay, too. Maybe partly because she's a mechanic? But that's stereotyping, and obviously it's not a given that all their friends would also be gay, and also she could be bi or pan or ace or literally anything and it isn't actually any of my business, except I'm curious.

"All packed up in here," says Terry. "I just left out a few basics that you'll need up to the last minute."

"I'm pretty close to done over here, too," says Scott. He's gotten the books all packed and is now using a screwdriver to take apart the bookcase itself. "It's good you got all these boxes from your work."

"Oh yes," says Alonso, "we're both getting laid off and the library's closing, but gosh, these sturdy Ingram boxes sure are handy!"

I haven't heard Alonso being sarcastic like that before—I guess he tones it down with Youth Council. I still can't quite believe the library's closing. Just a few weeks ago at Thanksgiving I told Uncle Dean he should pretend they were losing their jobs to make Grandma feel like they needed a place to stay and that she could help them. Now it's actually happening. It makes me feel like I somehow made it happen by saying it, even though that is clearly nonsense.

"Sorry," says Scott. "I just meant—"

"I know. It's fine."

"How are you doing, though?" asks Gail.

"We kind of knew it was coming. With the library, I mean, not everything with Dean's mom." Alonso has started carrying boxes out of the bedroom and stacking them up with the ones Gail and I have filled.

"Well, you got a good bonus niece out of the deal, anyway," says Gail, smiling at me. I blush, but in a not-embarrassed way.

"Yeah," says Alonso. "That's a definite plus."

IT FELT GOOD TO HELP ALONSO AND GAIL

and Terry and Scott pack up the apartment, but I still can't figure out what my job is in, like, a bigger sense. And it also kind of made me sad because, like Gail, I liked the apartment, and it seemed unfair that they had to give it up.

And then I felt like I should explain everything to Grandma about how Uncle Dean and Alonso were moving in—to help, but also to be helped, because they weren't going to have money coming in. But then I thought how that probably wasn't my job, either.

And then I was thinking about everything that happened at Thanksgiving, with the Pumpkin Palace and Dad wanting to pay for it, and Laura wanting me to move in with them, and I felt like I should talk to them, give them, like, an update. But I never call them. They sometimes call, but only for my birthday or Christmas. Christmas isn't super far off, actually, although I haven't thought about it at all except that PJ's probably visiting and that's like the one good thing.

Grandma's started keeping the TV on a lot. News, mostly, the kind where they just keep describing all the awful things that are happening everywhere. Every so often they break it up with, like, a lost dog finding its way home, or an invention that supposedly will make everyone's lives better, or an interview with an actor who has opinions about a cause. So there's never really a quiet space to try to put words into. And even if there were that quiet space, I don't know what I'd say.

I'm not sure Uncle Dean knows, either, but he's trying, right now. He just turned off the TV and is standing in front of it.

"Could you put the news back, please? I was watching," Grandma says. Snufkin is in her lap. He's been spending a lot of time on her lap lately. Maybe because she's not moving around as much?

"I know you were, Mom." I still haven't totally gotten used to Uncle Dean calling Grandma Mom, even though obviously that's who she is to him.

"I just need to let you know what's happening today," my uncle goes on. "We're going to be moving some stuff in, some friends are helping, so you won't need to—"

"How much stuff are we talking?" Grandma asks.

"It'll almost all be going into the basement, out of your way."

"Basement tends to flood, come spring," she says. "Could be a big mess."

"I remember," Uncle Dean says. "We got some pallets, they'll keep things a few inches off the floor. Should be fine. If it does flood, we've got the Shop-Vac."

"Well, don't be thinking you're going to have any big beer parties."

"No big beer parties, got it."

I find the concept of "big beer parties" hilarious and also think it's deeply unlikely that Uncle Dean and Alonso would have one, but I guess telling them that they can't is a way, maybe, that Grandma can feel more like she's in control.

TWENTY-EIGHT

ONE OF THE THINGS WE'VE DONE A LOT IN Youth Council that I always like is making displays and putting art on the bulletin board. Once we did a display of bug books and put up pictures of the coolest and weirdest-looking bugs and the books all got checked out right away. Another time we did a pet shop display where we took books about dogs and cats and hamsters and gerbils and snakes and lizards and put them in little cages we made. That one didn't work as well because people got confused and thought the books were somehow in jail and we were making a political statement, and we had to take it down.

Now that FPL is closing, I didn't think we'd be making any more displays. There are some things that have stopped already, like they canceled all their magazine and newspaper subscriptions, so the men who like to sit and read them all day are mad.

But FPL is going to keep doing programs until the literal last day, which is December 31, and Alonso says there's no reason we shouldn't decorate the bulletin board again, because "we'll be open until we're not."

We all want to know what will happen to the books and CDs

and DVDs and shelves and computers, and the rolling step stools that we like scooting around on, and the tables and chairs and costume box and storytime toys, and, of course, to the staff. (I mean, I personally kind of know what's happening to Alonso and Uncle Dean, but not all of it, not, like, what they're going to do for jobs. But I don't think they know that yet, either.)

And for a while today we were asking Alonso a lot of somewhat ridiculous questions, like whether we could just take all the books we wanted home and keep them forever, or if we could do a race in the stacks with all the rolling step stools, or if we could make a big sign that says CLOSING BECAUSE CITY COUNCIL IS DUMB and hang it over the library front door. But eventually we figured out—even those of us who aren't great with social cues—that our questions were making Alonso more sad than anything else, so we stopped.

So now we're doing a craft with some of the weeded books, the teen ones and some other ones that were in reference. Actually it's not totally a craft; it's a kind of creative writing thing, but it feels craftish because we're using markers.

Anyway, it's called blackout poetry, and it's when you make a new poem, or it doesn't really even have to be a poem, it can just be a new . . . arrangement of words, by blacking out or coloring over all the other words on a page.

Yesenia and Faisal make poems about their families, and they decide they want to take them home instead of putting them up. But they make some snowflakes for the bulletin board out of other book pages, and they come out pretty nice and, like, seasonally-appropriate-looking, even though it hasn't snowed yet.

Enrique is super proud of how he makes his blackout "poem" say *people can be so stupid seriously* using a page that was really about how words like *stupid* are offensive and people shouldn't use them, and when they do it should be taken seriously. "Not sure we can put that one up, buddy," says Alonso, and Enrique says, "I'm not saying people are *always* stupid, just that they *can* be, which is true and accurate. Shouldn't we want to post true and accurate statements?"

Linh makes one with no words from some Naruto pages; she does it so the only things you see are sad faces.

Alonso's making one, too. He doesn't always do crafts with us, and I look over to see what he's using. It's a page from something called the *Occupational Outlook Handbook*, and so far he's blacking out all the words on it.

The page I decide to use is from a book about metaphors, and I feel a little like I'm cheating because I'm using phrases instead of individual words; they're in all capital letters, and they're, like, statements. But they're the ones I want:

PROBLEMS ARE SOLID OBJECTS

LOVE IS A COLLABORATIVE WORK OF ART

"That's striking, Alex," says Alonso. "It makes me think of—there's an artist named Jenny Holzer. She makes art where she's often projecting words at a really large scale, like onto the sides of buildings. Why did you choose those words, if you feel like sharing?"

"Well, I don't know, maybe this is dumb," I say, "but I was thinking that if problems are solid objects and love is a collaborative work of art, maybe what you build love out of is actually problems."

TWENTY-NINE

"GETTING ALL READY FOR CHRISTMAS?" the Walmart cashier asked. Alonso smiled and nodded.

I want to tell her that not everybody celebrates Christmas, and she shouldn't make assumptions. But the fact is that we're buying wrapping paper with candy canes on it and a string of fairy lights and a fake tree that already has lights built into it, so it doesn't seem like the best time for that conversation.

We're also going to shop for presents for Grandma and Uncle Dean and PJ and cards for Dad and Laura, but I told him we should go to Faithful Angus for all of that because it's more interesting.

It's the first time we've gone places together, just Alonso and me. And part of me—the part that isn't used to Alonso being in my family—feels like this must be somehow related to Youth Council, like we must be out getting stuff for some program that's coming up, even though we didn't ever do that before, because, I guess, of the whole thing about not transporting minors.

I'm still a minor, but now I'm also a niece, which isn't something I thought I'd ever be.

I wonder how many other things I'll become that I don't know about yet.

***

FAITHFUL ANGUS IS AS CROWDED AS I'VE ever seen it, maybe because there's a lot of what a big sign labels as VINTAGE CHRISTMAS. It makes me think of the *Merry Christmas from the Eagers* card, which I think would qualify as an example of Vintage Christmas. There are a lot of cards and ornaments and wreaths and Santas of a style I can only describe as Terrifyingly Festive. Grandma and I are pretty low-key about Christmas usually, but I guess it's a bigger deal for Alonso. I found out some more about the rest of his family, parents and siblings and so on, when we were on the way. They're mostly in California, and he usually travels to them, but he won't be doing that this year, which I assume is because of it costing too much to get there, so I don't ask him why.

I find the stall where PJ and I got the photos the last time I was here, before the sleepover, before PJ moved, before Uncle Dean was Uncle Dean, before, before, before. There's still a big pile of photos in a wooden box, and some of them even look familiar, like I saw them the last time, too. I look for the old yearbook where PJ stuffed the KKK men, and I don't see it. I guess someone must have bought it. I wonder if whoever bought it has found the KKK men yet, and if they tore the photo up like PJ wanted to.

I start sorting photos into categories: pets, buildings, flowers, trees, people who look happy, people who look angry. I don't know what I'm looking for exactly until I find it.

I'm almost sure it's the same two women who were in the photo PJ got last time. They're both wearing these giant flowered hats that look cool in a there's-literally-a-parade-float-on-your-head kind of way, although they also seem like they'd be super heavy and would give you a headache. But anyway, the hats aren't even the best part. The best part is that they're looking at each other the same way they were in the photo PJ found, and in this one they're holding hands, too.

Now that I have the most important present, I can look for stuff for Grandma and Uncle Dean and a card for Dad and Laura. I wonder if I should get something for Alonso, too. I decide yes.

It takes me a while, but I turn up a set of wooden bookends shaped like rhinoceroses that I think go with the elephant-head key rack, which is now on the wall by our front door. I'm going to give one bookend to Uncle Dean and the other one to Alonso, which is maybe a little cheesy, but it also seems nice and couple-ish, and also, those plus PJ's present plus Grandma's take almost all the money I have, and I still need to track down a Dad-and-Laura card.

When I do, I find Alonso in the line to check out. "Don't look," I tell him. I've draped my coat over everything in my basket. "You either," he says. Then I'm extra glad I'm getting him something, because I guess he's getting me something, too.

The guy behind the counter is the same one who liked my shoes last time. "Hey, you're from the library, right?" he asks. For a second I think it's weird that he knows about Youth Council, then realize he's talking to Alonso, obviously. "I'm on the Friends mailing list," the guy continues. "I heard there are plans in the works to keep some things going?"

"I haven't heard much, but yes, I've been told that discussions are happening around tasks that volunteers might take on," Alonso says. "We'll have to see."

The guy must feel bad for Alonso, because when he rings him up, he throws in a big handful of the red-and-green-foil-wrapped Hershey's kisses from the silver bowl next to the register.

But then he does the same for me, so it actually must be just a general Christmas thing.

"Well, I've never been there before," Alonso says as we're buckling our seat belts. "Good call, Alex. I think of antique places as very spendy, but those prices weren't too bad."

"Yeah," I say, "I think they know nobody around here is, like, rich or anything."

We ride in silence for a little while, then Alonso puts on a Christmas playlist from his phone. I don't always like Christmas music, and some of it I really hate, but Alonso's is okay. I look at the photo some more, then at the scented neck pillow I found for Grandma (that wasn't an antique; they had some handmade-type stuff, too) and the card for Dad and Laura, which has a woodcut of a bird sitting on a holly branch, and what I like about it is that it was printed by, I think, a person and not like a big company. It's just red ink, and on the inside it says *Season's Greetings*, which I also like, because it's never *not* a season, so you could be greeting someone any time.

"Do my dad and Laura know about . . . everything?" I ask. Alonso has been singing along with the playlist. It made me think of Laura and how she was humming in a car with me, too, not that long ago and also forever ago, and also of Grandma, how when she sings, her voice is so strong and clear. I wonder what Uncle Dean's singing voice is like. I wonder if we'll ever all sing together.

He stops. "Your uncle has been emailing with Lucas—sorry, with your dad—"

"It's okay, I know what his name is," I say.

"Ha! Right, of course. So, your uncle has been keeping your dad in the loop, is my understanding, but quite honestly, I haven't pushed him for a lot of details on how that's been going. Has your dad reached out to you?"

"We don't do that much," I say. "It's mostly Laura who emails. I mean she always says *love from all of us*, but I don't think Dad is, like, super involved with writing the emails. And Liam and Logan are definitely not."

"Ah," says Alonso.

Laura did email me after Thanksgiving. She said everyone was glad to see me, and she was sorry it had also been a stressful time. Everyone hoped to see me again soon.

I didn't email her back, and I know that was rude, but I just didn't know what to say. So I'm hoping the bird-and-holly card will make up for it.

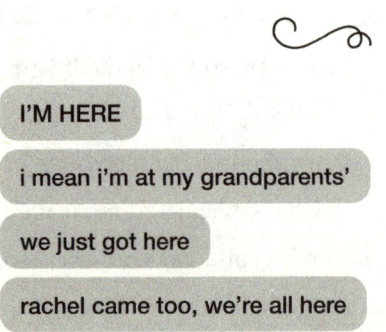

> for a whole WEEK

> !!!

I've just finished wrapping PJ's present—I put it in a plastic bag inside a box and stuffed the box with tissue paper so it'll take longer to get to it—and my hands are shaking as I type the exclamation points. I know it's a cliché, but she is the best present, and obviously I don't mean I think I, like, own her or something. But knowing that I'll actually get to see her gives me more of a holiday feeling than the tree or the lights, although they do look nice, and I think Grandma likes them, too. And Alonso and Uncle Dean and I made a lot of cookies. They have a cookie swap with a bunch of their friends—the ones I met helping get the apartment packed up and some other ones—and there have never been as many kinds of cookies in the house as there are right now. Alonso used all the Hershey's kisses we got from the antique mall to make peanut butter blossoms, except he used almond butter, which is better, it turns out. He and Uncle Dean are both good at cooking, and that seems to help make everything, I don't know, just kind of smoother? And we mostly eat at the table, now. All four of us. It's strange how quickly I've gotten used to there being a person for each chair.

But it's not all super great. The bathroom, for instance, is really crowded now. It turns out that Alonso and Uncle Dean have, like, a lot of hair products? And Alonso's hair, specifically, gets stuck in the drain and is gross.

And part of me is so glad they're here. But at the same time it's a constant reminder that Grandma isn't okay, that she's never not going to need help, that she'll need more, not less, as time goes on.

And it's never just me and Grandma anymore.

When Uncle Dean and Alonso first moved in, they put most of their stuff in the basement, and for the first few days they were sleeping down there, too. But it turns out that it gets really freezing at night, so they ended up moving everything out of the guest room that was Uncle Dean's room before and putting their bed and dressers in there instead. It's super cramped, but I guess that's better than cold. It still must be really strange for Uncle Dean to be in his old room, but maybe being there with Alonso, and with their own stuff, makes that better, too.

Anyway, their room is next to mine, and I was worried I'd hear, like, sex sounds, but so far that hasn't happened, thank goodness. I do hear their voices, though. Never loud enough for me to hear every word; I catch just enough that I get really curious, and then really mad when I can't understand.

And any time I want to do something, I have to basically get permission from Grandma *and* Uncle Dean *and* Alonso. If I don't ask Grandma first, then she gets upset, but even if she says yes, it's not a guarantee that Uncle Dean and Alonso will, too. (I can't call him Uncle Alonso; it just sounds weird. He said it's fine for me to keep calling him Alonso, but that if I wanted to add something, I could say Tío Alonso, which sounds better, like, the words go together more, but he's still mostly just Alonso in my head. But maybe that will change.)

The one who is most unbothered out of all of us is Snufkin. Now he has four warm surfaces to settle on instead of just two.

Alonso's a little bit allergic, so sometimes when Snufkin sits on him, it makes him sneeze. That startles Snufkin, but basically he either just runs away, finds a different lap, or, like, stalks in a circle around Alonso and then comes right back.

I start to type a new text:

when can we

And then stop. When can we what, exactly? Obviously I want to see PJ as soon as possible, and what I really want is more kissing the way we kissed in the ravine, right before she told me they were moving. I'm blushing but also still having the holiday feeling.

I've been in my room—"holed up," as Grandma would say—getting the presents wrapped, so I bring them all out to the living room to put under the tree.

The living room is different now, too, partially because it's Christmasified. The tree is sort of wedged into a corner, because we didn't want to make it harder for Grandma to navigate in her wheelchair, and also because, this way, if Snufkin tries to climb, it'll be harder for him to actually knock the tree over. There are holiday cards tucked into the branches along with the ornaments, an Alonso-and-Uncle-Dean decorating thing that I like.

And the futon couch that used to be in the kitchendininglivingroom of Uncle Dean and Alonso's cute apartment is in here now, too, facing the TV, behind the coffee table next to Grandma's recliner. Which makes the room pretty cramped and squished, but also sort of cozier?

Alonso moves a little closer to Uncle Dean on the futon couch to make space for me, but I stay where I am, kneeling by the tree.

The TV is on—not the news, to my relief. It's one of Grandma's mystery shows. The same one we were watching months ago. The same episode, even.

"That girl wasn't kidnapped," Grandma says.

"You don't think so?" Alonso asks.

"You'll see," she says.

I want to think she remembers watching it before, but maybe she doesn't. Maybe whatever makes her good at solving mysteries is still kind of working. Maybe there's no way to know.

An ad comes on for one of the drugs Grandma takes. I ask, over the serious voice reciting the long list of side effects, "Can I take PJ her present and some cookies? She's at her grandparents'?"

"They're having their family time. You don't need to be butting into that," says Grandma.

"They're here for a whole week, though! That's so much family time!"

"Hold it until tomorrow, Alex. It's past eight and it's crummy out," Uncle Dean says.

"You don't have to drive me. I can walk!" I say, although as I'm saying it, it occurs to me that I don't actually know exactly where PJ's grandparents live, and also that it is, in fact, crummy out. It was sleeting earlier, and now it's gotten colder.

"It's pitch-dark, and the streets are an ice rink. Not gonna happen," says Uncle Dean.

"Want to watch with us?" Alonso asks.

"I've seen this one," I say.

"Mysteries are better the second time," says Alonso. "You

know what's coming, so you can see how they set things up, notice what's in the background."

"You just hate suspense," Uncle Dean says.

"There's enough suspense in reality," says Alonso.

"She wasn't kidnapped," says Grandma. "She left. There was something the family wanted for her that she didn't."

"Huh," says Uncle Dean.

It feels like he's speaking a different language where *huh* means way more than it usually does. But I can't quite translate.

I could be very teenagery right now and stomp back to my room because I can't see PJ immediately, my holiday feeling turning to resentment like sugar going from caramelized to burnt.

But even besides the crappy weather, PJ and her moms did just get to her grandparents' place. And even though I know Rachel and Kyla, I've never met Kyla's parents, so it could be really awkward. And I bet PJ doesn't have her own room there; she's probably on, like, a couch or something with no privacy.

So instead of trying to butt into PJ's family time (that word always makes me think you'd be bumping into things with your actual butt) I sprawl on the floor with one of the big brown-corduroy-covered pillows Uncle Dean and Alonso brought along with the futon couch, and Snufkin settles on me, and I have what I guess actually counts as family time of my own.

THIRTY

THE PLAN WAS NOT A PERFECT PLAN. IT maybe wasn't even a good plan. But it was the best PJ and I could come up with after literal hours of texting. And surprisingly, all our various adults went for it, even Grandma. It helped that it got warmer again and thawed, so people weren't so worried about driving.

Tonight, Christmas Eve-Eve, otherwise known as December 23, we're going to have a winter-holiday-and-also-we're-sad-the-library's-closing-and-also-kind-of-the-going-away-party-we-never-had-for-PJ party. And we're having it at Vince's 24 Hours. Not everybody can come on such short notice, but Yesenia said she and her family can be there, and we'll see who else shows up.

This is why I'm standing in front of my closet right now, and why there are rejected outfits all over my bed.

My phone rings. I jump, look at the caller ID, answer. "Dad?"

Did something else awful happen?

"Hey there, Alex—merry Christmas!"

"It's the twenty-third?"

Dad laughs. "Yes, I'm jumping the gun some, but we're, uh, gonna be off the grid on the actual day, so I thought I'd wish my daughter a merry Christmas a little bit early. And, uh, also just wanted to check in."

This isn't a video call, so I can't be certain, but I'm 99.9 percent sure that Laura's right next to him and nudged him to say that last part about checking in.

"Off the grid?" I ask, thinking of graph paper and geometry.

"Out of cell range. We'll be Christmas camping!"

"Sounds cold."

"Not with the right gear! We'll have to get you out here one of these times—you wouldn't believe the stars, away from light pollution. Anyway, uh, how are you doing?"

"Fine," I say automatically.

"We're only off the grid for Christmas Day itself," says Laura. "Hi, I'm here, too; we've got you on speaker! And listen, you can still call or text, we just won't see it for a bit? But we'll be checking as soon as we're back in range."

"Okay," I say.

"And we wanted to say, too, that we're still here for you and your grandma. It sounds like things are holding together for the time being, but if that changes, we're just a call away."

Unless they're off the grid. I imagine all of Failin with grid lines hovering over it, the library and school and Faithful Angus Antique Mall and Vince's 24 Hours, the people like dots on a graph where you have to plot a curve's trajectory.

Laura's telling me my trajectory might still take me to live with them in Bend, and Grandma's might still take her to the Pumpkin Palace.

"Thanks," I say. "I'll keep that in mind."

"So mature!" Laura says. "Have a wonderful holiday, Alex. We'll be thinking of you."

"You too," I say.

"Bye now, love you," says Dad.

"Love you too," I say back, because it would be weird if I didn't.

Then I go back to the closet and take out my mom's dress. I get the wooden bird-head medallion and the shiny black oval stone with the hole in it from the jewelry box, too, and thread them onto a short silver chain that used to have a BFF charm on it until PJ and I decided that that kind of friendship advertising was weird and bad.

The wooden bird-head medallion and the shiny black oval stone clack together satisfyingly on the silver chain. The bird-head carving is rough, not splintery rough but just a complex texture, and the stone is super smooth. They're good fidgets. I can already see myself playing with them in stressful times. Or even just regular times, although I feel like it's been a while since I've had any of those. I wonder why it took me this long to take them out of the jewelry box to wear. I guess they didn't quite feel like mine yet. Now they do.

I don't know if my mom would have, like fashiony people say, *completed the ensemble* with rainbow sneakers and a black hoodie, but that's what I do.

WHEN I COME OUT WEARING THE DRESS,

Uncle Dean is the only one in the living room; Grandma and Alonso must still be getting ready. My uncle says, "Is that—"

"It was in the cedar chest," I say. It still smells of cedar, a little.

"Maybe warn me next time," he says, and for an awful second I wonder if my mom was actually wearing it when she died. But then he goes on: "You just look a lot like her, kid, a lot a lot, and I remember when she got that dress. I was with her. I think I got a shirt—yeah, it was striped, too; we always liked stripes. Secondhand Rose! Your grandma didn't like us shopping there. Haven't thought about that place in years."

"Why didn't Grandma like it?"

Why did I ask him about a store?

"Oh, she's not a fan of buying used. Or at least she wasn't back then. Is she now?"

"No," I say, and it suddenly occurs to me that as much as I want to know more about my mom, there was a long time when he and Grandma weren't talking, so he might want to know more about his mom, too.

And maybe it'll just take us both a while to tell each other.

IT TAKES LONGER TO GET PLACES NOW IF

we're all going, which we are. Grandma has a walker instead of the wheelchair, which has to go in the trunk because it doesn't fit anywhere else. Every time we're getting into Uncle Dean and Alonso's car, she asks about where her car is, and every time Uncle Dean "reminds" her it's in the shop. Which is a lie, but a lie that so far has been working. Tonight Alonso is driving, which Grandma seems to actually like better than when Uncle Dean drives, although I can't tell much difference between their driving styles.

"Sure is dark," Grandma says. "Drive carefully."

It is dark, and chilly, even though it isn't frozen cold, and probably I should have worn leggings or something instead of bike shorts under the dress, but I'd rather be coldish than too hot. The roads are pretty quiet, and it's nice to see the light displays some people have outlining their doorways and windows and roofs. Grandma has never wanted to mess with outdoor lights—too much of a hassle, she says. Maybe next year Alonso will put up some.

When we get to Vince's 24 Hours, PJ and her moms and two older people who must be her grandparents are already there.

I've been so excited about seeing PJ that I kind of forgot the adults would be seeing each other, too, and that Grandma will probably say something off, or get upset or restless or—

"Kathy Eager!" PJ's grandma says. "So nice to see you! It's been ages! You probably don't recognize me, but it's Molly Gibson, I was Molly McKee then—"

"Of course!" says Grandma, with none of the hesitation or confusion I'm expecting. "Afternoons and Saturday mornings. You were fond of those funny-tasting cordials, as I recall."

"Wait, you worked here? You *both* worked here? When? How come you never said?" PJ demands.

"Well, I guess it never came up," PJ's grandma says. "And yes! Rosewater cordials. Good memory, Kathy!"

I've read about this, how things from early life can be clearer than more recent things for people with memory loss. I don't really understand it, but I know there's something about pathways, and how the ones you form when you're young are, like, stronger?

Which makes me wonder if, decades in the future, I'll be able to remember exactly what's happening right now.

"Cordials!" says PJ. "We have to get some! We'll be back!" She grabs my hand and drags me over to the candy section. I mean, she doesn't have to drag me, but she's kind of yanking on my arm, which I don't mind.

"I didn't really want cordials," she says right next to my ear, which makes me go shivery. "I mean, I do, because obviously, but mostly I just wanted to be with you without anyone else around."

"That's not going to be easy considering how many people we invited," I say.

"Yeah, I know. It's awkward. There is something we could do, but you might think it's weird? I got the idea from my moms. They were talking about it during Family Dinner back at Thanksgiving. Apparently, when they were first together and needed a place to be, like, private, when they were out and about? They would sometimes"—she lowers her voice again—"hide in the bathroom."

"It does have a door that locks," I say.

"Exactly."

We take the long way around from the candy section so we don't have to go by the tables where everyone's sitting. We're laughing in that way where we literally can't stop, like just-opened shaken-up sodas, fizzing all over the place. But as soon as we're in the actual bathroom, we get extremely quiet. I lock the door and lean against it. PJ puts the toilet seat down, which makes it feel a little less bathroomish, more like just a small space with a sink and a mirror and a weirdly-shaped chair.

"Hi," PJ says.

"Hi."

"That dress is amazing. You look fantastic."

I smile, and I think for a second about telling PJ the whole story of the dress. But then she says, "I missed you so much," and then she's wrapping her arms around me, leaning into me like I'm leaning against the door, and everywhere our bodies are touching feels like it suddenly has a million new nerve endings. I hug her back, hard, then move my hands to the back of her neck to stroke her freshly buzzed velvety hair. I pull her face close, and finally we're kissing again, soft at first like we're making sure we still know how to get our lips to touch, then stronger, like now we've got the basics down we can work on figuring out the full potential of this whole kissing phenomenon, and I'm glad I have the door helping to hold me up, because I'm melting.

Then the door is shaking, and the knob is rattling, and someone, clearly, needs this room for its actual intended purpose, and PJ and I spring away from each other, instantly transformed back into shaken-up sodas. "I guess we should, like, leave now?" I ask, and she nods, and I call out "Just a second!" and fumble for my phone and quickly take a picture of us in the mirror, flushed and giggling.

Then I open the door: Yesenia. Who just says, "Hi, PJ! Hi, Alex! What were you even—"

"Catching up!" I say, my blush going to an intensity that I hope is beyond the visible spectrum.

"Okay, whatever. Do either of you have a tampon? And will you wait for me? It's still almost all adults over there"—she waves toward the tables—"and I don't feel like just talking to Enrique."

"Yeah, sure, I get that," says PJ, and the three of us crack up. Which makes me feel especially good because of how mad I know PJ was at Yesenia for a while there.

"I have some." I rummage in my backpack, find the pencil case I use for tampons, hand it to Yesenia. "Take what you need."

"Thanks!" She goes in.

"I can't believe so many people showed up," says PJ.

I realize Enrique's about to find out, or maybe he has already, that my "parole officer" is actually my uncle, and also that Uncle Dean and Alonso are a couple.

And I actually don't mind at all.

"And, like, we wouldn't all be here right now if all the bad stuff hadn't happened," I say. "I mean, not that you moving is totally bad, I guess, except I obviously wish you hadn't had to, but, like, everything with Grandma, and the library."

"I know."

We're quiet for the next couple of minutes, and then Yesenia comes out.

"Thanks for waiting. You know I haven't ever been here before? It's so cute!"

"Oh my gosh, then you don't know about the secret menu!" says PJ. "The secret menu is everything."

PJ starts explaining everything on the secret menu to Yesenia as we walk slowly over to join Grandma and Uncle Dean and Alonso; and PJ's moms and grandparents; and Yesenia's whole family, including Tía Gabi; and Enrique and his dad. As we get close enough to hear the conversation, Grandma's saying, "Sounds like things are still amphibious."

And I think she means ambiguous?

And I think she's talking about the library, probably?

After me and PJ and Yesenia find places to sit, there's a silence, which I hope is just because people are looking at menus and not because they're all thinking about how Grandma used the wrong word. I feel myself tensing up, getting rigid.

Then PJ's grandmother says, "Kathy, I hope you can help me out. Ever since we got here and I saw you, I've been trying to bring it back to mind—there was a song I liked that you used to sing, like an old folk song, maybe? And I recall the tune, I think, but not the lyrics."

She starts humming, and I know what it is right away. Grandma starts singing, and me and PJ join in, and after a minute, so does Uncle Dean. I didn't think he'd know it, but she must have sung it while he and my mom were growing up, too. I like Uncle Dean's singing voice, deep and warm. I wonder if it sounds like my grandpa's did, and if mine sounds like my mom's.

We sing about the mole in the ground, and then about the hole in the ground and the mountain upside down, and PJ's grandmother applauds. Then her grandfather sings a folk song he likes, and then everyone is chiming in with different songs and teaching each other verses, and who knew that this assortment of people would turn out to be a group that would sing together at a restaurant?

While I'm singing along with everyone, and being kind of astonished that I'm not embarrassed about the public-like-a-frog-ness of the singing, I also keep thinking about Grandma saying *amphibious*. Even though I still hate that she used the wrong word, something about it feels right.

Amphibious means something that can operate on land or in water, and it makes me think of how whether I wanted to or not, I've been learning to adapt to whatever happens.

Figuring out new ways to make things work.

Flowing.

The opposite of rigid.

ACKNOWLEDGMENTS

Mountain Upside Down has been a long time coming, and it means a lot to me. Both my parents suffered from dementia before they died, and the book was inspired in part by my grief. I love and miss my mom and dad and will always be grateful to them.

And this book wouldn't exist without the support of so many other colleagues and comrades, family and friends. Thanks to Michael Bourret for believing in me and in the book, and for your clear-eyed, astute perspective throughout the process of finding it a home. Thanks to Andrew Karre for giving it a home, for asking all the right questions and paying such close and generous attention to Alex and her community. Thanks to everyone at Penguin: publisher Julie Strauss-Gabel; interior designer Anna Booth; cover designer Kelley Brady; and cover illustrator Ana Vonhuben, who drew Alex and PJ the way I see them in my head—I love all the details you worked into the illustration. Thanks to managing editors Natalie Vielkind, Madison Penico, and Rye White; copy chief Rob Farren; copyeditor Brian Luster, proofreader Kat Keating; Vanessa Robles in production; and publicist Jaleesa Davis. Thanks also to Bri Lockhart, Amber Reichert, Lauren Festa, Carmela Iaria, Trevor Ingerson, Summer Ogata, Danielle Presley, Judith Huerta, Gaby Paez, and Venessa Carson from the school and library and trade marketing teams—much appreciation for all your work.

Thanks to everyone in my writing communities: to Scrivas past and present for all the feedback and encouragement; to Nisi Shawl for all the Zooms; to Jenn Reese for writing dates and talking me off ledges and for hosting such an excellent online watercooler and local. Thanks to past and present faculty colleagues, students, and staff in the Vermont College of Fine Arts MFA in Writing for Children & Young Adults; you are all so committed to the importance of writing for young readers and I learn so much from our work together. Special shoutout to Cory McCarthy for being excited about the book from the time when I was just starting to figure it out, and for consulting on all things swimming-related; any natatory errors are mine, of course.

Thanks to my library comrades for your dedication, flexibility, tenaciousness, and senses of humor. It's a challenging era to work in libraries and I'm glad to be in such good company.

Thanks to Hanne and Holt and all your animals, especially Bogle, for the oasis you provided in hard times. Thanks to Katie and Dylan for many years of friendship, and to Ramona for demanding stories and for almost always being excited to see me. Thanks to Victoria for infectious enthusiasm and for introducing me to so many things I never would have discovered on my own. And finally, thanks to Steve, for Steve knows what and Steve knows why. We're still getting away with it.